Love Lies and Drama

Lateka Forte'

DEDICATION

I dedicate my first book to my wonderful husband and darling children.

ACKNOWLEDGEMENTS

I have been up and down, had many trials and tribulations. But I know God doesn't give you nothing you cannot handle and he has always favored me. With that being said I will like to give thanks to God for everything he has blessed me with. He allowed me to do what I wanted to do in my life. Always put him first no matter what is going on. And I never would have made it without him. I also want everyone to know I have the best husband in the world, he supported me and encouraged me to do what made me happy. And he is my biggest fan. Thank you and I love you from my soul Mr. Forte'.

To my children Sa'nya and Jalen, mommy loves you and thank you for giving me silence during my writing time. My parents for giving me life and allowing me to be me. Thank you for encouraging me throughout life. I love you forever and always. To my sister Nicole, be strong and God has a plan for you. Your blessing is around the corner and you have been patient long enough. Thank you for believing in me and accepting me for who I am. I love you always.

My brothers Jermaine and Corbin, thank you for being by my side. I love you guys always. To my girl-friends who have become my sisters from another mother. Sabrina, Shella and Tiffany, thank you ladies so much for the positive energy, the motivation, great advice and shoulder to lean on I love you ladies forever! Thank you to everyone who have been and will always be a positive vibe in my life.

Lastly, and most importantly, thank you so much to Angela Stevenson for helping me reach my dreams. I had no idea what to do or where to go but you came into my life and this was easier than I expected. Looking forward to releasing more books under Alegna Media Publishing, LLC.

Chapter 1

Living in Atlanta has its advantages and disadvantages. I was born and raised here so I am an original Georgia Peach. I don't think I could ever live anywhere else! Now that I am twenty- three years old, I have my own condo in Atlantic Station. I decided at a very young age that as soon as I graduated from high school I was moving out. My parents were not rich but they provided the necessary things in life, which were food, shelter and clothes, but me being me I knew it wasn't enough. I had to have the brand names, the fancy cars, and the fancy home. I landed my first job right after graduation at this law firm in downtown Atlanta, I have been there for five years. They started me out with fourteen dollars an hour and at that time that was a lot of money for a high school graduate with no experience. I had just finished unpacking my last box at my new spot when I received my first visitor.

"Who is it?" I yelled out. *"It's me, Justice, your cousin girl"*! Justice shouted. Now Justice is my first cousin and we have been hanging for years, I can say she's my favorite cousin. One thing for sure, she doesn't take any shit from no one.

"Girl, I was just coming over to see your new place and to tell you what this bitch Kela did. Justice says, as she moves about checking out my crib. Oh, how nice, I like, I like. I know where I am going to be crashing some nights after the clubs. But any who, why this hoe Kela had the nerve to call me and say she going to kick your ass as soon as she sees you. She talking about her man told her you were trying to holler at him in the club last night. He only told her that cause one of her snooping ass friends told her she seen him in your face last night. Now we both know you were blowing his ass off but that's not how she heard it. I told Kela, Lacy is the last one you want to fuck with, she may be quiet but she doesn't take any shit. So she is talking about heading to your condo now because she knows where you moved." Justice explained. "Honey she can bring her stank ass on over here, I don't have shit to hide, I wouldn't give that nigga the time of day, with his broke ass and she knows it. Bitches kill me always believing a nigga before they can let the female tell the truth. But if she coming over here to fight, then it's an ass whooping she's going to get. I'm tired of them bitches thinking they can just fight anyone." I shouted. "Well that's why I came over because I didn't want those hoes thinking they can jump you; if she wants to fight it's going to be one on one." Justice says while snapping her fingers and rolling her neck.

I decided to show Justice the rest of the condo until those two bitches decide to show. From the living room, to the kitchen, then to the dining room, to the bathroom and then my two bedrooms, Justice was all Oh's and Ah's! She loved my place and was already talking about taking the extra bedroom. My condo was everything anyone could have wanted. Three levels, with decks on the top two levels, plus a two car garage. The view was amazing.

I was overlooking the heart of Atlanta. As I was still giving Justice the tour, all of a sudden we hear, *'Knock, knock, knock, knock" Loud* as hell! Of course, I looked through the peep hole and it was them, ugly and uglier! I politely opened the door and said "Hey, what y'all doing over here?" They were looking all crazy like I was supposed to be scared. "Well I have something that I will like to talk to you about, and I think it will be better said in person then over the phone." Kela said. "Well come on in and let's talk, I mean that's the least I can do since you came all the way over here." I said being a little smart ass. While rolling her eyes and waving her hands around, Kela started. "I heard you were in the club last night all in my man's face trying to get him to go home with you and I really don't appreciate it. After all, we are cousins right? I think you really crossed the line". I was taken aback by her statement. "Wow", I guess I can actually say you heard wrong. I am sure Justice has already told you what really went down but you didn't want to hear it. So there is no need for me to try to explain shit to you because you came over here with your mind already made up. If it's a fight you looking for, then I am letting you know now I'm not backing down to no bitch". I yelled while stepping up closer in her face.

Bop, bop, bop was all I heard before I realized this bitch just sucker punched me! It was on from there because those were the first, second and last hits she got in. I pounced on her ass like a lion in the jungle. Before I knew it we were all over the living room because she kept trying to run. My pictures fell to the floor and shattered in small pieces. I hit her ass so hard that she hit the floor. All I remember was seeing blood all over the place where her nose and her lips were busted. Then I stood up over her and started stomping her ass. She was hollering, "Get her off of me, get her off of me!" That's when Justice pulled me away and Kela's sister Mesha picked her up. Kela's face was bloody, she had a cut under her eye from my fist. She looked shocked! They ran out of my place so fast it was too funny. Justice was laughing so hard she couldn't stop, but me; I was still furious and wanted some more. My knuckles were sore and had spots of blood on them but it was well worth it. The nerve of that bitch to hit me when I turn my head, I can't believe that shit! But she got exactly what she was looking for. "Girl, I was going to let you beat her ass longer until she started screaming like a child getting a whooping from her mama, Justice stated, while doubled over from laughter. But let's clean her blood up and go shopping so we can hit the clubs up tonight." Still agitated, I reply, "That's cool, because I need to calm down anyway and what better way to calm down than shopping." While we were cleaning someone else started knocking on my door, I thought it was them bitches coming back for more, because the knock was the same way. When I got to the door it was the police, first thing I thought was this bitch called the police on me and she came over here with that shit. I opened the door and there stood two of Atlanta's finest officers I have ever seen. Mouth wide open I said, "Hello Officer's, how may I help you?" The tallest darkest officer spoke stating they received a call about a disturbance. I was so mesmerized by his sexiness that I was just standing there in awe. " Oh I'm sorry I had a couple of ladies over thinking that they were going to punk me in my own home and I had to handle my business, after all the whore sucker punched me officer." "Well you look fine to me." The officer said while taking a look at my face and body. He was satisfied with what he saw. "Just keep the noise to a minimum and remember that you do have neighbors that hear everything." The officer explained.

I let him know that we were on our way out and that there will be no more noise complaints from my place, unless I needed to see him personally. He was tickled by my bold statement and handed me his card with his personal cell on it and told me to call him when I was free. The other officer also handed me his card for Justice because he was interested in her. When they left we laughed so hard and shivered at each other. It's a shame that we have been blessed with so much beauty and sexiness. Justice and I come from a family where our skin is lighter than most. I am five foot six inches tall and I have a body shaped exactly like the old coke cola bottle. My waist is not too small and not too big, my skin is a smooth caramel color with hazel eyes that completes my beauty.

My natural hair is curly but when I have it pressed with a hot comb its silky straight. Justice on the other hand is the complete opposite of me. She is five foot eight, slim with more breast than she has ass. Her skin is more like a lighter caramel than mines, but also smooth. I always tell her she has a white girl booty. Her hair is shoulder length, but she likes to wear all these crazy weaves with different colors. The funny part is, no matter the color it fits her complexion. Her eyes are a beautiful, grayish brown, and the most amazing feature of all is her pearly white teeth. They create a beautiful smile.

No matter where we go, we attract all types of men, it's fun on some days but for other days we just like to have fun. Not to mention, that's how we get a lot of things we have. Justice is pushing a Mercedes s500 class, and I have a Jaguar. These cars were one of many gifts from our sugar daddies; all they want is a little time with us. In return, they take us to corporate dinners and show us off as their trophies to their upscale clients, we go on expensive trips, have luxury cars and unlimited shopping sprees. I do have a job, because this fantasy may not last long and I have to save the money I make for a rainy day. Now these men are sexy older guys, I could not see myself with someone disgusting. So we fuck occasionally just to keep them satisfied, and to keep the money and gifts coming regularly. The men are the type that has no family, always too busy to settle down, and they are always looking for the next youngest thing that understands and can keep them happy from time to time. Some people may call what we do as prostituting but we like to call it a favor for a favor. They get what they want and in return why can't we get what we want.

We left the condo for the day to do a little

shopping, we decided to ride in Justice's Mercedes since it is a convertible and because I left my car at my mom's house and road with the movers to show them to the condo. When we arrived at Lennox mall the parking was super thick, so we decided to valet park the car. After the fight, I didn't feel like walking too far, but we still managed to hit up all types of stores. People were looking at us as if we were celebrities. We are regulars at the stores in Lennox mall and the sale reps know us by name and always have the latest clothes for us to pick through. They never put them on the floor for sale until we have picked out what we want. I selected a lot of Jimmy Choo and Christian Louboutin pumps, they were to die for! All I wear are heels; the only pair of tennis shoes I own are gym shoes. Got to keep the body looking tight. After getting our weekly wardrobe it was time for us to head out, we had been in the mall for four hours and have bags to last a lifetime. Now it was time to go home and get ready for the club, after all it is a Saturday and it is hot. Justice car was loaded; the truck was full and the back seat. It was eight o'clock and we were headed back to my spot, Justice can get ready there and unload her things in the extra bedroom. When we arrived back it was dark, so I told Justice to park the car in the garage and we can unload our stuff from there. I don't trust no one in Atlanta, we can be unloading the car in front of the condo and get robbed, so I rather be safe than sorry.

Soon as we got everything out of the car, we began putting our things away. Justice had already taken over the second bedroom and to be honest I got the two bedrooms in hopes that she will consider moving in and covering half of the bills. "So Justice, what you think about making this your room permanently?" I asked her. "Well it is a nice spot and I see that I will have my own private bedroom, bath and a garage. But how much exactly will I have to pay because I would love to move in?" Justice asked anxiously. "The condo is one thousand a month and utilities we can split as they come because they are different each month. So for now I will say five hundred and utilities as they come. As you can see your room is on a different floor than mines, you have your own deck and both rooms are big as hell with large bathrooms. The kitchen and living room is on the bottom floor along with a guest bathroom as you have seen, so we each will have privacy when needed." I explained. Justice shouted "well it's settled, you officially have a new roommate, and I will get my bedroom suite moved in tomorrow and my clothes."   I was just too excited now, I like my new place but I didn't want to be arriving home alone in a city that never sleeps. At least with Justice here I can feel a little safer. I left Justice to her new room, she was on the second floor and I was on the top floor. We showered and got dressed and were ready for the club. Since it was June, I wore a pair of white shorts that came just below my booty cheeks with a white blouse with the back out and the front drooping, to reveal my cleavage. In addition, to top it off I had on a pair of my Christian Louboutin that were simmering pink and gold. Justice on the other hand, wore a strapless fuchsia body fitting dress that came just below her booty. Her pink and fuchsia Jimmy Choos complimented her dress. We are fierce and loving it.

Chapter 2

When we arrived at the club, by the looks of the line it was going to be banging that night. We pulled up to the front to valet park and all eyes were on us. The guys were checking and the women were hating. But because we are regulars at the clubs in Atlanta, we were able to do at least three clubs a night by just walking right up and the bouncers would let us in because they knew us. Club DREA was the most elegant club, the age limit was twenty five but of course we know people so we may have been the youngest in the club. The music was bumping, but this was the club we went to first just to try and get our night popping. We didn't stay long in this club because we felt like we needed to be a little more crunk in our night because of what happen earlier. Truthfully I was in need of a thug to keep me company. We decided to go to the one club we knew Kala and Mesha would be at. Once we arrived at

Club Central in Hapeville, I knew this was it for the night. The line was crazy long and this was the only place we could not get in as fast unless we paid extra, but that was not a problem because we met a couple of guys in the VIP line and they paid our way in. Once inside, Justice and I had already decided to have a few drinks with the guys that paid our way in then we would ditch them to find what we came here looking for. The music was on point, Pastor Troy, Lil Wayne, Chris Brown, Young Joc, Ludicrous and Lil Jon was off the hook. I danced and danced until I couldn't dance anymore. Justice started laughing which brought my attention to Kela and Mesha standing at the bar with their flunky girl crew. Kela face looked a hot mess but she tried to cover it up with make-up.

One of the girls with them, noticed Justice and me on the dance floor, so Kela and Mesha decided they all will walk over. "I guess you think this is over huh? It isn't over, because I will whoop your ass".

Kela stated. "Yeah just like you whooped my ass earlier, bitch please your face don't look like that for no reason. I kicked your ass then and I will kick your ass now, don't let the outfit fool you". I yelled and moved closer to her. "The only reason you got the best of her is because y'all jumped her". One of her flunkies said. Justice chimed in with her hand on her hip, "Who told you that? That's a mutha fucking lie, Lacy kicked Kela's ass and me and Mesha watched. I guess she got to tell you that since she thinks she is the baddest thing walking!" They turned around and walked off. Another ass whooping was the last thing Kela wanted. I can't believe she told those girls that we jumped her and that her sister was not there. That was too funny to see the look on her girls faces when the truth came out. Bitches will say anything to make themselves look good. We danced and danced until the club closed. We were on our way to the car when a couple of fine ass dudes approached us. OMG! Was all that I could say at that moment and of course I said it to myself. "Excuse me ladies, we were wondering if you wanted to go catch a bite to eat with us." One of the men stated. "And you are?" I asked. "I'm Tony and this is Black my twin brother. And we have been looking at you ladies all night, we didn't want to approach you cause we seen you come in with those dudes, but then we saw y'all ditch them too." Tony stated. "Is that so, well we were heading home but I guess we can hang out for a few more hours, where is your car? We can follow you to IHOP." I said. Tony and Black walked over to a sharp ass black two door Bentley that was parked a few cars down from Justice's Mercedes. Justice and I looked at each other and knew that we got what we came for.

We had already worked our plan out, Tony was mines and Black was hers, they looked alike because they were twins so the only thing different was their personalities. They were about six foot, chocolate as hell, firm looking bodies and can dress to kill. It was stupid packed when we walked in; it was like everybody from the club came straight to IHOP. We found a spot in the back by the window; Justice sat across from Black and I sat across from Tony. It was like they had also picked us too. "So, what do you gentlemen do for a living?" I asked not trying to be to nosey, but I needed to know. "Oh, we are entrepreneurs, handling our own business with international business clients and local clients". Tony stated. I can say very impressive cover up, so in other words they are big time drug dealers using different companies as a cover up.

Dealing with international dealers and selling to local dealers. I have the scope on everything. It pays to be book smart and street smart. "Well I work at a law firm downtown, and Justice here is a house wife, just without the husband, but we make a pretty good living." I explained. We ate, talked, and had a great time with them. Then it was time for us to go. Tony didn't want to end the night and neither did I. Justice and Black were all for keeping the night going, so we invited them back to our spot. I rode with Tony and Black rode with Justice.

When we arrived, we had already decided that this was something that we would take slow, because these gentlemen were some keepers, so no fucking tonight. I allowed Tony to park his car in the garage since my car was still not there. We all talked and laughed and got to know each other real quick, it was like I had known him all my life. Justice and Black ended up falling asleep on the sofa because her bedroom was not ready yet. I allowed Tony to sleep in my bed with me but we just cuddled and talked ourselves to sleep.

Chapter 3

Last night was great, exactly how I planned it. Found a nice spot to hang and then met a man I think I am going to enjoy sexing. It can only get better from here. While I'm at my parents' house, I figured I can sit around for a while since my sister Nikki is here with her kids. Nikki has four kids she started young. My parents were really upset when she became pregnant with her first child but they didn't believe in abortions, so at fourteen my oldest sister had a baby boy. And he was the most beautiful baby I have ever seen. His hair was black with silky curls and his skin was really bright. His dad was bi-racial, which of course made him bi-racial. Nikki's second child came at eighteen; he weighed 9lbs; 15 ounces; the baby had hands as big as mines. His father was different from her first baby, and is actually the father of the next three babies she had. Her kids are now twelve, eight, seven and three.

These kids were already beginning to tear through our parent's house. They were running and yelling. Throwing things and when I would yell for them to stop but my mother would say "oh they just being kids leave them alone." I remember being a child and getting my ass whooped every day for something I did as a kid. My mom had really mellowed down. She was cooking her usual Sunday dinner, which consisted of all these fatty foods cooked with grease and fat meat. I was not going to stay for dinner because I hated soul food at this time in my life. We ate soul food every day except on Saturdays when I was growing up and I hated every day of it. My sister loves it, she cook these big meals for her family everyday too. She is a house wife just without the marriage so she has the time to cook like that also. My youngest brother Carl was sitting in his room talking on the phone with one of the many women he met online or through one of the chat lines. I have never seen anyone meeting people by phone or internet; I have to see how they look before I even give them my number. However, that was his thing and he enjoyed it. I also have an older brother named Jay- Jay, he has spent most of his life in prison since he was a juvenile. That boy has been bad all his life, but you can't do nothing but love him because he has a genuine heart.

I started laughing when my sister said, "Sharon called me last night telling me about the fight you had with Kela. She said you kicked her ass all over your new spot." I laughed before saying. "I sure did, she had no business coming to my house accusing me of wanting that ugly man she call her boyfriend. Please I have men way sexier and cuter than him." My mom goes on to say "I told you not to be hanging around them girls, they ain't nothing but trouble. Always have been and always will be. They just like their momma." I shook my said. "Mother this I know, but I had to learn for myself. Now she sees I am not playing with her. She had the nerve to approach me in the club last night talking about it ain't over. From the looks of her face it was over long time ago. I am just waiting for her to bring it again." My mom looked at me real serious before she spoke. "You know we're going to hear about this later as soon as grandma and your Auntie Sand find out. They gonna be saying you shouldn't have bet that girl the way you did."

What was I to do? Just sit there and let that bitch just hit me and do nothing about it. Please I don't care what anybody got to say about it because I was defending myself and I will just cross that bridge when it gets here. Well I decided it was time for me to leave and get ready for my dinner date with Tony. "Well Mother and Nikki, I guess I will see you gals next Sunday. I have a dinner date with this very sexy chocolate brother I met last night in the club." My mother looked at me and said "Lacy, you need to make sure you protect yourself out there in those streets. You a single beautiful lady and these men just want to get in your pants. So you be careful." Moms are always over protective of their children but I can handle myself very well. After all I don't carry a 38 revolver for nothing. I am always packing my lifesaver in my car and purse. I have a permit to carry it wherever I go. I kissed the bad kids goodbye and headed home to take a nice relaxing bubble bath before I started my night.

When I got in my car, my seat was moved so I knew my brother was driving my car. I will deal with him later. I popped my X-scape cd in the player and rode to the sweet sounds of their voices. Those girls can really blow. I lip sing the whole time I am driving, just enjoying the scenery. Atlanta is so beautiful in the day but at night, it is gorgeous! I decided to cruise through downtown instead of taking the expressway. Just riding downtown on Peachtree Street brought back memories of me catching the number thirty-one bus to get to five points train station. I went to Booker T. Washington High School, which was across town. I did not want to go to my home school, which was Southside. I had to be different. We would go to Underground Atlanta after school just to hang out a few hours before the transit bus came to take us home. The people are out on this Sunday. Looks like a bunch of tourist. I rode Peachtree Street all the way to Seventeenth Street where I entered my garage and parked my car for the night. Justice was not back yet from dropping me off earlier. I set the alarm because I feel safer with it on. I made sure I text Justice to let her know the alarm was set.

I did not know what I wanted to wear that night. He had already seen me in my sleek yet hoochie outfit. It was time for me to bring it down a notch. I decided on a black pencil fitting dress from Prada that came to my knees. The dress is strapless but I also have a wrap that I can wear with it. I think my black and red Prada pumps will go well with the dress. The right perfume for the evening and the perfect make up will complete my outfit for the night. I decided to wash my hair and wear it natural. My hair is very pretty natural and it answers most men questions when they see me with my hair pressed. And that is always, yes this is my hair. Women in Atlanta wear a lot of weaves, but if a man runs his fingers through my hair he will feel my scalp without the lumps. Okay I have everything in order, now it is time to run my bath. While my water is running, for my bath, my phone rings and it is Tony. Lord please tell me he is just calling to confirm tonight and not cancel. "Hello" I said in my sexy voice. "Hey beautiful, I was just calling to let you know I will be running a little late tonight. So, instead of me picking you up at seven, I will be there no later than eight. I just wanted to be sure that was okay with you." Tony stated all sexy. "That's fine, as long as you are not cancelling on me. I will see you at eight." I told him. We hung up and I continued to stare out the window at the view. I have not put any drapes or blinds up in my room. I was enjoying the view in the mornings and at night. Once my water was complete, I looked at the time and Tony changing the time was good for me because seven o' clock was just an hour away. I was going to need an hour in the tub. Before I knew it, I was sound asleep in the tub. I was out for about an hour and a half when I awaken to my cell phone ringing. It was Tony. Oh my God, it was eight o'clock on the dot and I was not dressed yet. I answered only for him to tell me he was at the door. I quickly got out the tub put on my robe and raced downstairs to let him in. I explained to him "Sorry, I am not dressed yet just give me a few minutes and I will be ready. I seemed to have fallen asleep in the tub." He was tickled by what happen to me and I politely gave him the remote to the television while I pranced upstairs to get ready. It only took me about fifth teen minutes to get myself together and we were out the door. We arrived at this restaurant located on top of the Hilton hotel in Atlanta, the view was even more beautiful than my condo. We were seated in a private room that was overlooking the north side of the city. Tony was a complete gentleman. It was just amazing how he spoke French to the waiter and ordered some Crystal' for our table and to keep them coming until I did not want anymore. I did not understand French but Spanish was my second language of choice since it is mostly needed in Atlanta. I am just thinking this guy pushing major weight in the drug game and he knows everything so far. Dinner was great. We talked about our lives and where we saw ourselves in five years. I ordered the lobster and shrimp smothered in Crab Creole cream sauce and he had the lobster and steak. It's amazing how we like the same things in life and have plans for a family with kids. After dinner, we drove to his spot in Alpharetta. At first, I thought we were just riding, but when he entered the code to the gate, I was in awe! This big ass home and not to mention the ten acres it sat on was beautiful. He had told me at dinner that he had to pick up some things at his house and wanted me to ride with him. When I walked inside the house, it was as if I were with some type of celebrity. The mansion had hardwood floors, marble countertops, stainless steel appliances. There was a bar with a poolroom, basketball court and anything else you can name was there.

I waited in the den while he gathered the things he needed. Then he said to me "If you don't mind, I would like to drop these items off without you. Can you stay here till I return? It shouldn't take me longer than an hour." I agreed since I didn't have anything else to do and I did not want this night to end. I made myself at home while he was gone. I fixed me a drink and started watching television. I was fast asleep on the sofa when he arrived back home. He must have been gone quite a while. He woke me up and showed me to the bedroom where I fell back to sleep in his arms. This is what I like about him. He does not pressure me into sex, it's like he wants to take it slow also. When morning arrived I was awaken by the smell of breakfast and was starving. I noticed my dress was gone and I was wearing one of his t-shits. All I could do was smile about it. I went downstairs to find him sitting behind a table full of food and he extended his hand for me to take a seat beside him. "Good Morning, beautiful." He said to me. "Good morning, I didn't know you can cook." I said shyly. "I can't I have a chef, she just left a few minutes ago, I thought the least I can do is have breakfast made for you." He replied. I laughed and started picking through the food I wanted to eat, then I realize, it's Monday. I'm supposed to be at work. I politely excused myself from the table so that I could call out for the day, because it was no way that I was going to make it. I returned to the kitchen and continued to eat. He had apologized for leaving me alone last night and for coming back so late. I was okay with it because I had fallen asleep in thirty minutes anyway.

He asked me to stay longer but I told him I needed to shower and change clothes. He insisted that I shower there and he will have the boutique down the street bring some clothes for me to choose from. I had no choice but to agree, so after breakfast I showered and put on a robe he gave me and when the lady from the boutique arrived, I knew her from the many times I spent in her shop. She immediately informed me that she had my weekly clothes on hold at the boutique and will be right back with them. He laughed at me, he knew then I was one of the many divas in Atlanta. When she returned, I picked through the clothes and decided on the clothes I would keep; only this time I did not have to pay the bill. Tony paid the bill and insisted that I did not have to pay him back. I am more and more impressed by this man every day. I got dressed and we just stayed in his house playing different games and watching movies. The day went by so fast and I was kinda' sad like a kid leaving Disney World when I had to go home.

Chapter 4

When I got home Justice still wasn't there, now I was starting to worry. Where was this chick? And why haven't she called me? I checked her room but it was the same way she left it that Sunday. So I decided to call her but she did not answer. I left a message "hey Justice, what's up? I haven't heard from you or seen you since yesterday. Hit me up and let me know you okay." Hours went by and still no answer from her so I did what I had to do, and that was to call my Auntie Sand to see where she was. After talking to my Auntie, I learned that Justice had went to see Kela and Mesha and was arrested after she jumped on Kela. I can't believe she had to fight Kela right after I did. Supposedly Kela was talking about pressing charges against me and Justice went over there to talk her out of it and Kela got in Justice face so Justice hit her and hit her until the police came. She could have at least called me I would have handled Kela again. But since Justice beat her up she can't press charges against me now because she can't prove it, her previous bruises was covered up by Justices new licks she gave her. I also learned that she was given a bond this morning so I decided to drive over to the Fulton County jail and bail my cousin out. When I walked outside, I noticed Tony still sitting in his car. So I walked over and asked him if everything was alright. He assured me that everything was okay he was just on the phone and didn't want to pull off right then. I told him about Justice and he took me to the jail to bail her out. He mentioned it's not good for a lady to go to the jail alone, a lot of weird people walking around. Once I posted her bail they said it would be a couple of hours before she is released. Tony and I went back to the car to wait. He surprised me when he said, "I want to be honest with you.

I was still sitting in the car because I was

trying to figure out, how I can come to your door and kiss you since I have not kissed you all weekend." Then he started kissing me. His lips were soft like butter and this man's kiss was amazing. He put his tongue in my mouth and sucked my tongue too. I was in heaven; at least I thought I was. I could feel my clitoris rising and ready for what was next, but I knew I had to take it slow. He was a keeper and if I gave it up too soon he may look at me differently. So kissing was something that we can defiantly do daily. I don't know how I ended up straddling him in his car but we were into this kiss. The way he was kissing me with the passion was turning me on and on. I can feel his dick pressed up against my leg and I must say it is long and thick. I am going to enjoy him when the time is right.

We toned our kissing down and I got back in my seat. "That was a nice kiss." I told him. "Nice?

That's what you call a nice kiss? I need something like amazing or one of a kind." He told me as he rubbed my leg. I laughed and said "You're right, it was one of a kind and amazing. I just want to know why you are single? It's obvious you are the total package." He laughed and said "I have never met a woman that can match me. Most of the women I meet are gold diggers and only want me because they see the type of car I drive.

Many of them are already near someone in the game and look for single guys like me, thinking they can just get right in. But that's not me, you know; that was my first time at Club Central, my brother and I decided we would try a different approach. That's why it took us all night to talk to y'all. However, I see that the last thing you need me for, is money, cause you make your own, you have your own spot and car. I admire the way you dress and the way you carry yourself. You are the woman I have been searching for. You a hustler just like me. So I suggest them men you got giving you money you need to get rid of cause I need to be the only man in your life and I can supply you with all you need." I was impressed by his comment. "I thought you just said you did not want a woman after your money? And what makes you think I have men giving me money?" I asked him. He smiled at me and said, "I know you are not balling like you balling working at the law firm, I do have some common sense. And a pretty lady like you, I know there is a man or two giving you whatever you want however, I want to give you whatever you desire. And I know you are not after me for my money, because if you were we would have fucked the first night I met you." I can say he knows his shit. "Well what plans do you have for us since you want me to do all of this?" I asked because I need to know where I will stand with him. I was not going to cut off my cash flow for just a friend. I have about $80,000 saved up in my savings account, but I wasn't going to be living off of that the rest of my life. "I want you to be my lady; I mean I am not asking you to sleep with me because of that. We can still take it slow, but I want to be sure that you can commit yourself to me just as I can commit myself to you. So, I guess I am asking you if you would be my lady? A man like me needs a companion to keep me company during the night and on the weekend when I am not working." I told him okay I can do that and he kissed me again. I know these kissing will eventually lead us to the bedroom. We were interrupted by Justice knocking on the window. She had finally been released and was looking a hot mess. "Girl, how you know we were in this car picking you up?" I asked her. "Because I recognize the car from Saturday night, remember always remember the tag number to the car your girl riding in just in case you gotta' give the police some information." She said laughing. She got on in said her hellos to Tony and we took off. While riding in the car, Justice was telling me about how she ended up in Fulton County jail from that bitch Kela.

"Girl Mesha called me talking about Kela tripping. She mad because you whooped her ass and because I told her girls that we did not jump her. So I told Mesha put Kela on the phone, and of course this scary hoe gets on the phone talking about she gonna call the police on you and press charges because you attacked her in her home. So I was yelling at her, telling her Kela you know that's a lie you came to Lacy's spot trying to regulate and you got regulated on. It was a fair fight and that's that. So I told her I am on my way over there.

When I get there, she talking all this mess about she already called the police and they are on their way, so I told her I was gonna wait and tell them the truth and told Mesha she better not lie with her. Then Kela put her hands on me trying to push me out her apartment. I told her if you think Lacy kicked your ass then you better know I am going to beat your ass if you don't keep your hands off of me. Girl then she put her hand in my face and pushed my face back. All I heard was "Justice No!" from Mesha, and it was over. I hit her ass so hard in the face she fell back; I got on top of her ass and just kept hitting her in the face. That's when I heard the police telling me to freeze. It was over then. But the police told her she can't press charges against you because she has no proof due to the bruises she just got from me." Justice explained. "Honey I am not worried about Kela, if she know what's best for her she better stay out my lane. I'm just glad you okay. I will get one of the lawyers to defend you. They will get you off because she put her hands on you first" I told her. We had to take Justice to the impound to get her car because she didn't trust her car in Kela's parking lot. After we dropped her off at her car, Tony was looking like wow, and then he said, "She wild huh? Her and Black is gonna hit it off just fine because he is the wild twin. I am the calm one. But I didn't know you were a little feisty too, fighting right before the club Saturday. I don't recall seeing any bruises on you that night." "And you won't! I interjected; she didn't stand a chance when she walked in my condo. She did sucker punch me three times back to back and that was all she wrote. I tore in that ass." He was satisfied with the choice he made with me being his lady. I think he needs a woman that can hold her own down. He dropped me off at home and we called it a night. I did not ask him to stay because I had a long day ahead of me tomorrow.

Chapter 5 (Justice)

Damn I can't believe I got another damn charge. I hate going to court and paying these lawyers to keep me free. I mean there has to be another way. I just hate I let Kela get me to that point. Oh, well the bitch should have kept her hands to herself. I guess she will learn one day that Lacy and I can't be touched, point, blank, period. "NEXT," the rude ass clerk said at the towing company. I hate coming to these places. All they do is over charge you to move your car up the street and in their nasty ass impound. "Hey, I'm here to pick up a two thousand and ten Mercedes that was impounded yesterday." I said through the speaker. The clerk looked at me, smacked her teeth and said, "Do you have the tag number or VIN?" I was about two seconds from coming over that counter and whooping this bitch's ass. I hate how they act all hard behind these bullet proof glasses and bolted up doors, knowing if any one of their customers had the chance they will kick they ass over here. "Yeah it's P-A-I-D-4-E-V-A, PAID4EVA." I spoke to her through the speaker. She searched for the vehicle like she was mad because I was paid. All I could do was laugh to myself because I knew she was hating. After paying two hundred and sixty dollars to get my car back I was pulling out the gate and heading back to the house so I can shower and hit the streets.

My phone was left in my car, so I had many missed calls. Lacy called several times and Black called. I wasn't surprise to see that he called because we were supposed to hook up that night but all hell broke loose at the cousin's house and I was in jail for a day. I had already seen Lacy so there was no need to call her back, but I knew I had to call Black and let him know what was up. Tony had already said he was not going to tell him, that was my job and not his business. I can appreciate that from him. I dialed

Black's number and he didn't answer. I left a

message to call me back so I can explain about

yesterday as soon as he had the time. I got home in

no time that was the beauty of living in the city;

everything was no more than ten minutes away from

each other. I parked my car in the garage and

headed up the stairs. I just knew Lacy was with Tony

but when I got in the condo, she was fast asleep in

her room. I didn't bother her. I jumped in the

shower to get that jail smell off me, ordered some

wings and watched television for the rest of the

night. I just couldn't go out I was too tired cause I

didn't sleep all night. My phone rung and I thought it

was Black so I answered without even looking at the

caller ID. "Hello" I said in my sexy seductive voice.

"Bitch who the fuck you trying to sound all sexy for?"

Mesha said through the other end. I looked at the

phone and shook my head. I snapped back at her, "I

know the fuck you ain't calling me after that bullshit

you and your bitch ass sister pulled. I can't believe Kala acting brand new to the streets and calling the police after an ass whooping. What the fuck Mesha? Now I got to go to court to fight another case because she mad." Mesha was laughing in the phone and said. "Justice you know good and damn well I ain't got nothing to do with Kela. I told her stupid ass not to call the police but she's mad because Lacy embarrassed her in front of her girls and feel like she has to pay her ass back. I mean we family we suppose to fight and let that shit go but Kela on some other shit." I was surprised at Mesha she usually takes her sister side but I guess enough was enough. Kela was always the type to keep up shit. She stood on a high horse she could barely climb on and looked down at the rest of us. But when Lacy and I started showing up and showing out on her ass, she didn't want to hang with us anymore. Oh well, no love lost! May the baddest bitch succeed! I was hanging with

Lacy because she was prettier and much smarter than Kela and we were getting it in. I talked to Mesha for a few more minutes and then we hung up.

It was after eleven and I can't believe Black hasn't called me back yet. He was probably mad because I stood him up. But if he would call me back he will know the deal. RING......RING.......RING.......RING......RING......RING.... I must have fallen asleep because I was woke up from my phone ringing off the hook. I looked at the caller ID and it was Black, he must have lost his mind calling me this late, it was three in the morning. "Hello" I answered sleepy yet curious. He was whispering in the phone and I can tell he was up to no good. "Justice, I need you to come and pick me up. I was handling some business and got caught up. My car is blocked in and it's not safe for me to try and pull off in it at this point. I'm in the bluff, on the corner of Ashby and Simpson standing on the side of a house.

Pull up from the east side going to the west and I will jump right in." he said before disconnecting the call. He didn't even give me time to respond. I jumped up put on my shorts and jacket and my tennis shoes cause I didn't know if I was going to be running later. I pulled up to the corner and Black jumped in the car and we pulled off. He directed me as to which way to go and drove right past the spot he came from. I could see niggas looking and yelling. I could tell Black had pissed some people off.

"What the fuck is going on?" I asked him. "I killed that nigga and now they trying to figure out who did it." Black looked at me and said. "What? I can't believe you had me pick you up after that shit." I yelled at him. "Don't worry about it, them niggas didn't see my face or know me, this is what I do. The car I drove was a throw away car. It's not registered or nothing, but they had it blocked so I had to flee on foot and I couldn't risk them seeing me walking down the street. I wouldn't put you in a situation that I couldn't handle. Now this shit right here need to stay between us. Not even Lacy should know. I got your back long as I know you got mine," He explained. I was shocked but turned on at the same time. I mean what kind of shit did Lacy and I get ourselves into? These men were sexy yet dangerous and they were definitely paid in full. I smiled and said. "I got you, I understand. I was wondering why you didn't call me back. I wanted you to know that I did not mean to cancel our date but I had an altercation with my stupid ass cousin and landed myself in jail. Lacy came and bailed me out." Black looked at me smiling then started laughing before he said "girl you have to watch your back at all times, jail is not the place you want to be. I got to teach you how to whoop a bitch ass and don't get caught. But I understand, family know you anyway, so that was a lost situation from the first punch." I know exactly what he was talking about. We drove for what seemed like an hour making sure nobody was following us and ended up at his house in Alpharetta. He told me his brother lived next door but next door was like five miles away. We parked in his garage and went in the house. I followed him to his basement where he had a collection of guns, all types. It looked like a gun show in his basement and I was starting to wonder about him. I wasn't scared of shit but this nigga had me spooked. I had to ask, "What the fuck do you do for a living to be having all these guns? Are you a hit man? I am not with that crazy mess." Black looked at me and said, "Do I look like I do dirt for other mutherfuckers? I do dirt for myself and my brother. I have to protect the family business and let these niggas know we are not to be played with. All this shit you see are throw aways, the gun I used tonight is a throw away. It will never trace back to me. Are you ready to be in with this shit? Cause I need a woman that is ready to ride and die for me. I'm tired of all these bullshitting ass women who scared to even come down the steps. But from what you saying I can tell you hold your own and that's what I need. I can protect you and love you at the same time."

I was a little shocked by his comment and I have to admit I have never been with a man that was willing to protect me and I can't be that shocked if I came down here with him and picked him up. It was something about him and I just knew I had to keep him. We went upstairs and he showed me his place, his house was huge and I have never seen one this huge before. We laughed and this nigga had the nerve to say, he was getting ready to take a shower and I should join him so we can fuck. I was surprised at his boldness but I had to admit he was sexy and I was horny as hell.

We ended up in his shower kissing and he

grabbed me and placed me on his shoulder with my pussy in his face. He sucked and sucked on my pussy until I cum all in his mouth and he dropped me back on my feet in the shower. He was rough with the sex and I loved every moment of it. Black bent me over and entered his long thick dick in my pussy and began to work it. He was fucking me so hard I thought I was going to faint. Then he pulled me up and I straddled his dick in the shower. I showed him I wasn't scared and was not running from his dick. Hell this was the best dick I have had in years. We both came at the same time. We finished showering and hit the bed for round two. I woke up the next morning and my pussy was throbbing. I guess it was going to kill me the next day. Black was gone from the bed so I figured he was downstairs in his army room. That's the nickname I gave it. I cleaned up and put my clothes back on... and headed down so I can let him know I needed to get home to change clothes. I went downstairs and Black was nowhere in sight.

I wonder where he could be. Then I noticed him outside on the back deck talking on the phone. I tapped on the window and waved good bye. He signaled for me to come out and wrapped up his phone call. "Hey baby" he said while giving me a hug and a kiss. "Are you getting ready to leave?" he asked. "I am, I need some clothes and I have to go see this attorney about my case today to see if he can get it tossed out since it was self-defense." I explained to him. He grabbed me around my waist and pulled me closer to him and said. "Well why don't I come with you and I have an attorney that is sure to have those charges dropped and I will pay for it all. I like a woman that can handle her business but it's the least I can do since you came through for me last night." We decided it was best if I drove my car home and he would be about an hour behind me giving me time to get ready and we would ride in his car.

I left and arrived home within thirty minutes, Lacy was not there. She was spending a lot of time with Tony. I showered and put on my sexy look because I knew Black was the type of man that liked his women looking fine when he was out with them. My only hopes is, I will be the last of his search. I wore my skinny denim jeans, a silky royal blue tank, my black blazer and some royal blue pumps to compliment my tank. Black had called and said that he was around the corner, so I decided to stand out front and wait for him. Before he pulled up, I noticed this black van sitting across from the condo. I didn't pay it any attention, probably some new neighbors I thought. Black pulled up and I jumped in. We pulled off, he admired my style and I must admit I admired his too. I look in the mirror and noticed that this van was following us. "Black have you noticed that van that was sitting across from the condo is following us? Do you know what that may be about?" I asked him still looking in the mirror. He didn't turn around and look; instead he glanced in the mirror and noticed the van driving three cars behind us. "Naw baby, I didn't see that van because I was too busy looking at your sexy self, but let me go ahead and lose them without them knowing. Justice put your seatbelt on and hang tight." He said while still looking in the mirror. I put my seatbelt on and Black entered the expressway, it was a clean getaway since he was driving this fast ass Telsa Sports Car.

We snatched off so fast the van didn't have a chance. We pabout three exits up and he called Tony. Once he got off the phone, he told me he was still taking me to the attorney's office to see about having my charges dropped from beating Kela's ass. He would also be spending a lot of time at my place to see what's up with the black van. We didn't see the black van any more after that hectic day. Months later, I beat the charges Kela had against me since she didn't show up at court. Black and I have been spending day and night together at the condo and Lacy has been at Tony's spot. We've been doing all kinds of shit together. Me driving while he killing niggas. I just feel like this is not the life for me. I don't know what I should do about this. I love him and I know he loves me but this may be moving too fast and if this nigga get caught I am going down with him. If Lacy knew half the shit we doing she will be pissed at me. How did I end up with the gangster brother and she got the mellow one. Life is so unpredictable.

Chapter 6

Today marks the three-month anniversary for Tony and me. During these three months, he has shown me so many different ways a woman can be wined and dined. We have not slept together yet, but I think tonight will be a perfect night. I am so tired of masturbating after a heated date with him. I think it's time my pussy juices get licked and I feel his thick long dick inside of me. I have planned the perfect evening; I had the chef prepare us the same exact meal we had on our first date. Since it was September, I decided to have a nice warm fire in the fireplace and I had plenty of fruit for dessert but I planned on being his dessert. I decided I will have him lay down on the blanket in front of the fireplace while I excuse myself to the ladies room. Then I will come out dressed in a sexy ass lingerie that I purchased from Frederick's. My phone started to ring and my vision of our evening was interrupted.

"Hey baby, how's your day going?" I ask. "It's going well, I was checking to see how long you need me to be missing from the house while you set up this special surprise?" Tony asked. "Well I was thinking about a couple more hours I am almost finish." I explained. We said our goodbyes and I continued to work on my plan. The chef was almost done with dinner so the only thing I had to do was set up the fireplace and the living room, then take a nice shower.

The shower was great and everything is ready. I put on this sexy white see through lacy dress with a red bra and red thong to match. I was leaving little to the imagination. Tony walks in just as I finished setting the table. "Damn baby it smells good in here, I see what the surprise is, you." He said laughing. "Well, well, well I see you got jokes baby, but I am one of the many surprises you getting tonight. Go ahead and wash up and I will be waiting for you at the dinner table." I told him. "What's the occasion for me to deserve something so nice and surprising?" he asked. I told him, "Don't tell me that you forgot three months ago on this date we had our first date and became a couple." He responded by saying "okay I won't tell you." He went upstairs, took a quick shower, and got comfortable for the night. I played some slow jams while we ate and talked. Dinner was perfect, he enjoyed his lobster and steak and then I walked him to the living room where we sat in front of the fireplace talking and cuddling. Once the maid was finish with the kitchen, I walked her to the door and made sure we had the house to ourselves. I surprised him with a gift that I knew he had been looking at. It was a Rolex with ten-carat diamonds in the face and on the band. He was in shock and so happy I got him such a great gift. I was not expecting a gift since he said he forgot, but then he presented me with the matching Rolex and a five thousand dollar shopping spree card through visa so that I can go to any store I want. I was too excited when he gave me my gifts. I did exactly what I had planned; I excused myself from the living room, dimmed the lights and went in the bathroom to change my outfit. I changed into a red lingerie set that pushed my breast up higher than before, the lace trimmed my ass and the laced see- through top stopped right above my belly button and showed my belly ring. Then I topped it off with some red pumps, with my red lipstick. When I returned to the living room, I asked him to sit in the chair that was in near the fireplace. I could tell from the erection in his pants he was turned on by what he saw.

Once he was in the chair, I gave him a little strip tease show. Slowly removing my bra and panties, then I seductively took off his shirt and pants. He wasn't wearing any underwear, he never does. I begin to kiss him slowly on the lips and then his neck. He was grabbing my waist and kissing me softly as he always does. Then I removed his hands from my waist and dropped down to the floor where I started stroking his dick in my hand. His dick was huge and was the prettiest dick I have ever laid eyes on. I had to taste this one. I kissed his dick slowly and wrapped my juicy lips around it, then I began to go up and down and all around on his dick. He was moaning and I was moaning, his dick tasted so good in my mouth. I sucked his dick like I was sucking a chocolate ice cream bar. Then he took my body and flipped me upside down and starting licking and sucking on my pussy. This man had pussy eating and licking skills. I was cumming all in his mouth, but he sucked my juices like nothing was there. He then laid me on the floor and got on top of me and started making love to me. It had to be love because this was not an ordinary fuck. This man was kissing me and grinding his dick in and out my pussy. I was loving every moment of it. I then got on top and rode his ass until he cummed. I bet he ain't never had a bitch take a ride like that. Before I knew it, we were both knocked out in a deep sleep. I had finally gotten what I desired and I am sure he was very satisfied. We were awaken by the ringing of my cell phone. I thought I had turned that damn thing off. I grabbed my phone in hopes that it will not wake Tony but it was too late. I looked at my phone at it was a blocked number and I noticed the time was two o'clock in the morning. I was wondering who the hell could be calling me at this time. "Hello, Hello, Hello!" I answered. No one said anything on the other line, so I hung up.

My phone started ringing again and this time when I answered, I heard a lot of noise in the background like music and again no one said anything so I hung up. I decided then to turn my phone off and not let it disturb the rest of the night.

Tony got up and we finished the night off upstairs in the bed. I loved being at his house, it was so huge I felt like a queen. I spent most of my days and nights at his house now and Black spent most of his days and nights with Justice back at the condo. I was having the time of my life with this man and did not want it to end. By morning, I was well rested and Tony was gone, he left me a note that read:

Hey beautiful, sorry I am not able to see you get up this morning but I had to run and do some errands. Last night was amazing and I was hoping we can do it again real soon. I probably won't return until later today, so if you don't have plans for yourself today, just make some. I will talk to you later. And I think I am in love with you! I do hope you feel the same.

Oh my God, I would have never thought that he will be the one to say he loves me first, I mean it's nothing wrong with that cause I have been feeling that way for a while now. But I did not want to scare him off by telling him that. I guess I will call him later and chat. In the meantime, I'm sure if he is handling business that means Justice is free. It's time for me to catch up with my cousin and see what's been going on in the family. I took a shower first, got dressed, and drove over to the house. I decided to wear my dark denim Dereon jeans and a sexy blouse to match with some pumps for the day. I had to make sure I set the alarm before I left, for some reason Tony is very strict about the security surrounding his home; and we always have to park in the garage, he said if anyone ever tried to come in his home unannounced they would not know how many people are inside. This is true, because his house has five garage doors in which two cars can park in each one. When I pulled out the gate, I noticed a black van parked down the street, which is odd because no one lives at least a mile away. I was immediately put on alert when I passed the van, I pretended like I didn't see it. I called Tony to tell him about this but he didn't answer the phone so I just left him a message just in case I forget later when I talk to him. The fall weather was beautiful and I was enjoying every moment of it. I took the GA highway 400 south to 75/85 south to get to my condo in Atlantic Station. I lived only about forty-five minutes away from Tony's place.

When I arrived Justice was home alone like I suspected, Black had left earlier that morning also. "So what's good with cha chick?" I ask. Justice went on to say "Girl nothing just tired as hell, that nigga Black keeps a bitch on alert. The sex is on point and we doing it two to three times a day when he here." I was laughing at what she said and I told her "girl at least you know if you giving it to him he can't be getting it anywhere else. Anyway, I wanted to see if you wanted to hang out today? Tony had something to do and being that Black is gone too that means that they are together. So you game for hanging or what?" Justice looks at me and smiles then rolls her eyes. "Yeah I guess we can get out in the scenes since we haven't been around lately, I bet Kala and Mesha thinking we scared to come around. I heard there's a family barbeque at Grant Park." We decided to go to the barbeque and see what's popping off in the family now. I checked my mail while Justice got dressed. I decided I may need to change into some tennis shoes. Since I did not own any tennis shoes, I put on my Dereon t-shirt and told Justice we have to make a stop so that I can buy some tennis shoes for the park.

She laughed at me because she knew what I was thinking. When we pulled away from the condo, I noticed the same black van that I had seen outside Tony's house and now I begin to get paranoid. I said to Justice, "Don't look back with your head, just kinda' act like you checking your make up in the mirror and adjust it towards that van. I saw that same van outside Tony's spot this morning when I left to come here, now they sitting right there. I wonder if something bad is going on. I need to call Tony again but he is not answering." Justice checked the mirror and said "Girl I see them, they turning around look like they are going to follow us. We just need to play it normal and keep an eye on them. Try to lose them. And the other day when Black picked me up there was a black van that followed us but he jumped on the expressway and took off."

I turned before they could turn around and immediately make a few more turns until I ducked my car off in between some buildings. We saw them drive by on the next street slowly looking for us. Once they were out of sight, we got back on the road going back towards the condo and jumped on the expressway. We had lost them and now it was time for Tony to explain his business to me. If it's something that has my life in danger I need to know.

And why didn't that van follow him out this morning when he left. As I was thinking, I received a call from him. "Hey beautiful, I got your message and I am on my way to the house now. Are you okay?" he asked. "Yes I'm okay now. But that same van that I saw outside your house was outside the condo. They must have followed me there.

I went inside waited for Justice to get dress and then we left but I noticed the van. They were following me, but I ditched them without them knowing what I was doing. We heading to the shoe store now so that I can purchase some tennis shoes. Is everything okay Tony?" I asked. "Everything is okay, just as long as you are safe. It's not safe for you and Justice to be riding around. When you finish at the store, come back to my house I will be here with Black. We have something we want to discuss with you ladies. But first, I need you to rent a car with tinted windows and then take your car to your moms. Once you do that I need you to come to my house coming the front way. If you see the van; don't slow down or pull in. Just keep riding and I have a secret entrance that no one knows about. Once you get near the front call me and I will guide you to that entrance. And Lacy, I just want you to know I love you." He explained. I was nervous but I answered with "okay, and I love you too."

Once we hung up the phone, I explained to Justice what we needed to do. Once we walked in the shoe store, it was packed but I needed a good pair of running shoes that was stylish just in case. We didn't know what was going on or what was about to go down. I purchased a cute pair of tennis shoes to match my outfit and Justice purchased a pair also. We did exactly what Tony said to do. We went to the rental agency and rented a GMC Yukon because that was the only vehicle they had with tinted windows. I dropped my car off in front of my moms. I didn't have time to go inside and they were not at home anyway. So we took the expressway to Tony's house. And the black van was there, I called him and kept riding like nothing was wrong. He guided me to the back of his house where some bushes revealed a gate that opened. We pulled the SUV in and parked it in the garages in the back. While on the phone he informed me to be very quiet, do not say anything until we get to the lower part of the house. Just to be safe. So once inside and we were taken to this isolated room that was like a totally different house. "We did not wish to have you ladies in this situation like this, Tony said, but it seems that some people have surfaced and are trying to set us up. And before you can say anything let me explain. Black and I are from Miami and we got into a situation there.

We used to be in a mafia family there called the Lordels, we really did not have a choice to be in this family because our father was the King of the Lordels. Our home was ambushed when we were twelve and our father was killed. We escaped safely with our mother only because one of the many men that served our father and his family helped us. My father knew the attack was coming and had already planned for us to relocate to Atlanta. No one knew of his plan but my mother. She was given an alias identity that was set up and no trail of this was ever found in Miami. My father made sure that he covered his trail because he wanted to protect his precious family. After fleeing we started over here in Atlanta, we knew not to call back to Miami because our father was dead and our identity may be revealed. This is my home Lacy and Justice you have been to Black's home. Our mother is still alive and she lives in her own home nearby. She is protected around the clock by men that we recruited for her.

We visit our mother daily to ensure that she is

still safe and okay. My dad got into a real bad drug deal with the Mexican mafia and they sent a message that his whole family must die. But just like this secret room we are standing in, we had one in our home in Miami also, that was how we escaped. There was an underground tunnel that lead us to a boat. We are not drug lords or dealers, I am sure you probably suspected that we are. We are actually business men, my father wanted us to finish college and that is what we did. We now invest in different things to keep the money level where it is and beyond. My father left us with a great deal of money, he was a billionaire, and we are set for life. Our father dealt in drugs and the money is drug money. In order to cover up where the money was coming and to validate our income, we became investors.

We had an investment in Miami right before we met you guys and I believe that we were noticed by someone and they called the Mexicans to inform them. I know it has been over fifteen years since we left but the Mexicans declared war and wanted our family dead. And they will not finish until the last three members of the Lordels are dead. We have been investigating our father's death also because it was said that his body was never found. That has lead us to believe that he may still be alive and just in hiding or being held against his will in the Mexican dungeon. We asked you ladies here because you too may be in danger for dealing with us. I assure you we had no idea this was happening, we thought that shit in Miami was buried. The black van that you saw outside my house and your condo was also spotted at Black's house. That means we can't go back to your condo, my house or Black house. We are going to leave out the same way you came in and take you ladies to our mother's home until we find out what is going on. Her home has not been discovered by these people. This is only for a few days until we find out who is in the van. I am sorry to have brought so much information on you ladies but I felt you needed to know for your own safety."

Chapter 7

Once we arrived at the twin's mother house, it was just as big as their home. These people had major money like he said. His mother was not black, she was Panamanian with silky long black hair. She was beautiful and I can see the twins look just like her. They must have gotten their color from their father. Their mother was a diva, she was fashionable and looked like age did not play a part in her life. I was mesmerized by her beauty. I must have been staring for a while because then his mother spoke. "Come in, come in, it is a pleasure to meet you ladies. I have been asking Tony and Black to bring you ladies around. They did not quite tell me about you, but I can tell they were seeing someone they care deeply about. Maybe even love. And before you boys say anything to me, I must tell you a mother knows." She spoke with such elegance and her alias name was Lillian. We sat around for hours with her just talking about the guys when they were boys and how they loved their father. I could see a little darkness in her eyes whenever she mentioned her late husband. Time had gone by so fast and it was time for us to call it a night. Lillian had prepared two separate rooms for us to share with the guys. Tony and I were at the very end of the hall. Black and Justice were placed in the middle of the hall. Their mother resided in her master suite that was located on the third floor. This house has three floors and a full size basement. I was almost tired but I knew Tony was feeling horrible. I decided then that he needed to release some of the tension that was building up.

As I lit the candles I turned to the CD player and put in my slow jam cd. I removed his shirt so that I can massage his body so that he can relax. As he is laying there, I slip out of my jeans and t-shirt revealing my black panties and matching bra. He starts kissing me gently from my forehead until he reached my lips and then we exchange passionate kisses. At that moment, he laid me down on my back and licked every curve on my body sending exciting chills through my body. While he's licking my body his hands run down to my inner thigh till he hits that spot. My legs immediately spread open like he pressed a button. He then licked my inner thigh until he finds my sweet spot. While licking and sucking, I begin to shiver and shake; I caught my nut but he doesn't stop there. He licked and sucked me until my second orgasm came and my eyes rolled in the back of my head yet, he still continued as if I wasn't satisfied at that moment. I began squirting like a faucet. He then licked up my belly letting his tongue lead to my nipple. He gently placed his mouth around my breast sucking them slowly. I glided my hands down his chest to his stomach, and then I find his man hood at attention and ready to play. I make my way down till I find his soldier ready for action then I wrap my mouth around him taking him completely in. The sensation stimulates his body as I bob up and down on his soldier, his toes curl as I take him in completely, his eye's begin twirling as he begin to erupt. He then picked me up off the bed and placed me in his special place. My nails are in his back as he is nibbling on my ears and I am riding him. The noises I make makes him go deeper, we change positions as he place my head in the pillow, I bite the pillow while snatching the cover, he slowly strokes and pleases me in way's only showed in the movie's. He pulled my hair with his left arm and grabbed my hips with his right, I buckle as I have erupted but catch myself because I want more. He speeds up knowing that his volcano is about the erupt, I arch my back as I am and at that moment we erupt together causing what can be described as an earth quake. We both passed out on the bed because making love the way we did was a job of its own.

I was awaken by Tony the next morning, he had breakfast made and brought mines to me in bed. Sometimes I feel like having this man is too good to be true, but hearing his history and the loss of their father makes me understand better why he is the way he is. I was enjoying my breakfast then I heard the doorbell ringing. Tony jumped up and looked out the window. There was a black stretch limo outside, he was startled because he could not believe that his mother was going out. Before he made it to the door of the room, we heard a loud scream. At that point, Tony demanded that I stay there in the room. He grabbed his gun and rushed downstairs.

Being stubborn, I was not going to stay in that room without protection, for all I know this nigga can get into a gunfight and lose and I will be left up here to be killed. So I followed to the top of the steps where I saw Mrs. Lillian passed out on the floor and this man standing over her that looked just like the twins. Tony spoke, "Mom, mom can you hear me? Are you alright?" Mrs. Lillian begin to wake and was shaking her head in disbelief. It was their father and he was not dead after all. "We thought you were dead, no calls no nothing from you. How did you know where to find us? And what happen to you?" Tony asked. "My sons, and my beautiful wife, I have a lot that I have to explain to you. Could we please go sit down and talk, I know I have to explain and I am here to do that." His father said. Tony, Black and Lillian went into the family room, but no sooner than they went in Tony and Black came back to get me and Justice. They wanted us to hear what happen so that we will understand their life better. Justice sat next to Black on the sofa, I sat next to Tony in the chair while their mother and father embraced each other on the loveseat. I can see in her eyes that she still loved him and he was even more in love with her.

The way they touched and gazed into each

other eyes showed true love. Then their father spoke. "First off, I just want to say that I am happy that I was able to find you safe and living life happily. I had a few of my men follow you guys to see if everything was okay. I want to apologize for that. I see it only placed you in a tense mood. I feel I owe it to you guys to know how my life ended up like this. When I was younger, my mother was married to my father who at that time was the mayor of New York City. He would beat my mother and have her cover it up when guest arrived. He threatened my mother repeatedly if she thought about leaving. Finally, one day someone tipped the press off that the mayor was abusing his wife. It was then that my mother had the courage to leave without him knowing where we went. Because my father was our sole provider, my mother was able to get a low-income apartment in Queens, New York. It was the dump of all dumps but we had nowhere else to go. It was there in Queens that I found the drug industry. At eight years old, I was selling dope for one of the biggest kingpins in the state. My mother was not aware of what I was doing because she worked day and night in hopes of saving enough money to get us out of that place. She didn't seek any support from my father in fear that he will find us and kill her like he said. I saved the money that I earned from my hustling job and by the age of fifteen I was a millionaire." As their father spoke Justice was at full attention. I was in awe and had my ears on alert to make sure I didn't miss a thing. "That's when I decided my mom had worked long enough and before I could tell her we were moving out of Queens, I received the news that my mother had been murdered. The police claim it was a robbery gone badly but nothing was taken. She still had her purse and the twenty dollars she carried everyday with her. I knew then that my father had kept his promise." His eyes glazed up when he mentioned the death of his mother. I can see that he was still emotional about it. "I refused to go back to my father's so I did what any teenager would do that was in the game. I hit the streets even harder; my mother's death made me the man I am today. With family, I am all hearts and protective but with nigga's on the street I am ruthless and I spare no mercy. At eighteen, I received a message that Mr. Mierez himself, wanted to meet me because he wanted to know who I was. He admired my hustle and learned that my block was always on point, never short and was his highest selling block. I was on edge because I did not trust anyone. Mr. Mierez is your mother's father, he was a king pin himself. When I walked in his mansion I spotted your mother going up the stairs, she was mouth-dropping gorgeous and I knew then that she will be the woman that I fell in love with and will have my children. I was escorted outside to the pool where Mr. Mierez was sitting and we talked business. He wanted me to head to Miami and start a new organization there, he had heard that Miami was booming and he wanted part of the action. I was offered sixty percent of the proceeds since it was my life on the line and I was to only to send him forty percent back. I agreed, hell I was young and I was already rich, but what could be better than being richer. After speaking with Mr. Mierez I was headed to Miami.

I packed a bag to go down and peep the scene out. I was able to purchase a Mansion just as big as Mr. Mierez and I learned that Miami was thirsty for some of that good stuff we were offering in Queens. I didn't know anyone in Miami but I needed a few good men that I could trust. Therefore, I decided I had to bring at least half my block down with me to help recruit. After checking Miami out I was on the next flight back to New York, I had to let Mr. Mierez know that I had everything in order and was ready to go. I arrived back at his home without calling and your mom answered the door. She was so beautiful and I was speechless. I had women throwing themselves at me but I knew it was about the money but your mother she gave me the hardest time ever. I asked her out about ten times before she finally said yes." Lillian and he chuckled at each other at that moment. "Of course, I had to clear it with her father.

He wanted the best for his daughter and he admired my boldness and knew that I would be a good man for her. We dated for about three months then I left for Miami to relocate for good. I couldn't go without her so I asked her to marry me. We ended up in Miami and we were enjoying our life now as husband and wife. There was nothing that I wouldn't do for your mother. Business in Miami was booming and we were getting paid. Within a year we had took in ten million dollars and six million belonged to me and the other four million to Mr.

Mierez. The next year we took in three times the first year totaling out to thirty millions dollars. Only to find out that year that I did not need to split the earning with Mr. Mierez because he was killed in a brutal home invasion. Some of his men set him up and stole all the money he had at his home. His wife was killed which was your grandmother. It was heartbreaking for your mother, she took it very hard." Tears streamed down Lillian face at the mention of her parents. "However, she knew if she was not with me she would have been in the house and would have been murdered also. All of her father's estate was granted to her and we combined his millions with the millions we already had and became billionaire's. It was then that I realized what if this happens to me, how can I protect my family? I then began to have a tunnel dug to the nearest oceanfront and had a boat waiting at all times. I did not hire contractors in town because no one near you can be trusted. I had people coming from California to work on this tunnel. I knew if the same thing happened to my family I would not be able to live with myself. I was prepared to die because that was the life I chose for myself but I did not want your mother or you guys to get caught up in my mess. Because you can't help who you love, you just do. After the tunnel was built your mother became pregnant and we were proud to be future parents. I promised your mother at that time that I will get out of the game. I asked her to give me some time. I knew it was going to be hard but I had to do what was right so that my family can live a normal life. Years went by and it became harder and harder for me to let the game go. But as I watched you boys grow I knew I had to do it. I made one last drug deal that was going to secure my family as billionaires for life and life after. This deal was going to secure my men as well. I was getting involved with the Cubans and I was clueless to what they were doing." He stood up and began pacing back and forth as he continued his story. "I had a few men think they would try to cross the Cubans without my order and that started the war. Even though I punished those men the Cubans still believed that I called the order and put a hit out for my entire family. That's why I sent you guys away through the tunnel. I received word that you guys were safe and had your new identities. It was then that I set out to get revenge on the Cubans. I had to make them believe that I was dead so they would not expect what was coming to them. I had the home destroyed and left behind bodies from the morgue that were identical to my height and size and all of your height and size. I had to make them believe we all were dead. I did not contact you because I did not want anyone to know that we were alive. I could not trust the Cubans. It took me years to finally track down the exact location for them but I did. And I did what I had to do. I researched their every move for two years. I was able to get in and out with the job I did. I don't regret what I did because I knew the safety of my family rested in my hands. After returning to America, I begin searching for all of you. I looked for you under the names I provided but nothing was found. I then decided I needed to find the richest people in Atlanta because I knew you boys would be smart enough to stay rich. That's why you seen the vans parked in front of your houses and it explains why they were following you ladies. I had to be sure that you were my family. I have to admit Lillian, changing the names again was a great idea. The person that helped me with your identities could have turned on you easily. I miss you guys so much and hate I missed watching you grow up. But from the looks of things I can tell that you boys handled your business very well and your mother did what she had to do also. I am so very proud of all of you. And I want you to know that I apologize from the deepest spot in my heart for putting you through this mess in the beginning. I just always wanted the best for you so that you will never have to worry again."

I looked around the room and saw that everyone was in tears from the story that their father told. It was exciting yet heartbreaking. Tony and Black hugged their father for a long time. I can tell that they have been waiting for that explanation all their life. "So does this mean I can finally go back to my condo to change clothes?" I asked. They looked at me and laughed. I'm just happy it was not the Cubans that were following us. "Yes you can go back to your condo and my place." Tony stated proudly. I gave Tony a big hug and kiss while Justice and Black embraced each other as well. "Well Mr., I'm sorry I did not get your name." I said. Their father responded with "young lady I apologize my name is

Charlie and if you insist on calling me Mr...... then you may address me as Mr. Charlie, if that is okay with you." "Oh, yes sir, it is just fine with me, I believe in giving respect and Mr. Charlie it is. My name is Lacy and this is my cousin Justice, I must say it is a pleasure and a relief to finally meet you. If you are anything like your sons I think we all will get along just fine." I stated.

Mrs. Lillian showed Mr. Charlie around their new home and they look like the love was never lost between them. Tony and I left with Justice and Black right behind us. When we arrived at Tony's house the black van was gone and everything was in place like we left it. Justice and I were able to get in the rental SUV and head out to our own spot to relax for the day. The guys had some things they had to catch up on. When we arrived back at the condo, we were just in disbelief of what we had just been through. Being followed, having to rent a truck and go through a secret entrance. It was very stressful and that's what made Justice say what she said next. "I think I am going to leave Black alone, I can't deal with a life of secrets and wondering if I am going to be next on anyone's hit-list. The only reason I stayed around was because I had no choice it was either stay with them and be safe or get killed is what I thought. I mean I like him a lot but my life is more important than dealing with a man with all this baggage." She stated. I was in shock at what she said and I was thinking that she was in love with Black like I was in love with Tony, but they have had their problems and haven't been as close as Tony and I. So I asked her, "is this something that you just figured out or have you been feeling like this? And when do you plan on telling Black? I just can't believe you will just be so quick to call it quits. I don't feel that our life was in too much danger, they were willing to protect us at any cost. I know we have never been through anything like this before but I just feel safer with Tony. But I know you have to do what you feel and if that is how you feel, I just suggest you let him know as soon as you can." Justice was looking out the window and I could feel her pain. She was actually scared and this is the first time I have seen her like this. She played it cool while we were with the men but she has really let go now. "I plan on telling him as soon as I can, but I will call him and break the news. I am afraid of what he will do if I tell him face to face. But I have to wait till I move my things out from here. I wanted you to know too that I will be moving out I don't feel like this place is safe anymore. I will continue to pay the rent until you decide what you want to do, and I will appreciate it if you would not let him know where I have moved too." Justice explained. I was in shock, she's moving out. "Justice I completely understand your situation and I have no problem with you moving out. Just cover this month rent and that's all. I am actually thinking about selling the place now and relocating. I may move in with Tony for a while until I can locate another place. He asked me to move in with him before all this began but I didn't want to leave you here all alone. I can help you pack your things now and when you leave I will greatly appreciate it if you call Black and explain to him your position, you at least owe that to him." I stated. We laughed and went upstairs to Justice's room and started packing. This girl has tons of clothes and should have paid someone to do this for her. We packed and packed and laughed about good times. I knew this would be the last time I see my cousin for awhile so I was making the best of it. Once we were done, Justice put her suitcases in her car and left. She was sending some movers back next week to get the rest of her things. It was just me again. I decided this rental was way overdue and I needed to return it to get my baby back. So I locked up the place and headed downtown to return the SUV, then I remembered I left my damn car at my mom house. I arrived at the rental company and was able to get a shuttle from there to take me to my vehicle. Traffic was horrible during this time trying to get to the Grant Park area. The driver was a young black man and he tried to holla' at me. Did he really think I would give him the time of day? Hell no! I politely told him that I was in a serious relationship and he don't like the thought of me having friends. The driver dropped me off in front of my mom house and I knew they were not at home. I jumped in my Jag and pulled off. I'm surprise my seat hasn't been moved. Guess my brother did not take it for a ride. On my way back to my place my phone started ringing and it was Tony. I answered, "Hey baby, what's up?" He sounded a little upset and told me "Hey beautiful, I just left Black and he seemed a bit upset. Justice called him and told him that she was not into all this mess and felt a lot safer if she just left him alone and he left her alone. My brother is all messed up, he talking about doing some crazy shit. I had to send him home. But I was calling you to see if you knew what was going on, so I can calm his ass down later." I knew it was coming but not this soon Justice did not waste any time doing what she had to do. I was happy she did, so no feelings can go on any longer. "Well, when we got back to the house she was really scared, she held herself together while we were there, but when we got home she told me that she was not able to live life like this. She even moved out. I helped her pack and I told her to promise me that she will tell Black as soon as she can. I hate it happen but I understand her position. I'm glad she told him." I stated. Tony was a little upset over the phone he couldn't believe it. I could hear it in his voice when he spoke again. "I just think it's bullshit, my brother was really into Justice, she just don't understand. He has never been under a woman like he was with her. He was even telling me he was ready to be committed to her. I know him and all he wants is happiness, he may have a loose temper but deep down he's ready for romance." Tony explained. I pulled up at the house and noticed Black standing in front of the condo. "Hey, I'm home now and it looks like your brother is at my door." I stated. "I'm on my way." Tony shouted. I opened the garage and parked my car inside; I didn't close the garage because I did not want Black to think I was avoiding him. So I was walking towards the front door when he met me in between. I can tell he was furious and at this point, I was a little scared of what he might do, so I soften the ice. "Hey Black, What's up? Justice moved out!" I explained. He looked even madder. Then he started to speak, "Yeah, I figured she would not be here. Did she tell you where she was going? Or do you even know why she feels I would let anyone hurt her? I fell in love with her and I can't believe she would just walk away from what we had. We may have fussed and bullshitted each other, but she was the only woman I have ever been this close too. I just can't believe she would just walk away." I can tell that Black was emotionally upset; I didn't want to say anything that would hurt him any further. "I am so sorry about this, I had no idea. Justice has always been a tough girl and I thought the little commotion would have been exciting to her, but I guess inside she is still human and feels it too. I think she loves you too, and if you give it some time or give me some time, I can call her, talk to her, and see if this is something she really wants to do. I know you may be hurting, but I think she is hurting even more. We have been waiting years for guys like you and your brother to come into our life. I just know she needs time, she may have been spooked by the situation, I mean we were followed and almost ran off the road."

I explained.

Before Black could say anything else, Tony pulled up and I was happy. I didn't know how much more I can say to him to make him feel okay. Tony jumped out the car and looked at us. "You alright man, I been looking for you." He asked Black. "Yeah I'm good, I just came to talk to Justice but she moved out. I will just call her later. Lacy, thanks for the talk and let me know how she's doing from time to time." Black stated. "I will Black and everything will work out in due time, you be careful." I shouted. Tony and I watched as Black pulled off and we headed in the house. I made sure I shut the garage. I can see that Tony was upset at his brother. I was not aware what his brother was capable of doing but I knew Tony knew and that's why he rushed over. "I can't believe he came here after I told him not too, she's gone and he has to respect that. I want you to get your things and come back to my house. I just feel like he is going to return because he doesn't think Justice moved out this soon. I don't want you in the middle of this. Can you stay with me for a while until this blows over?"

Tony asked me. "I was actually thinking about selling this place and taking you up on your offer from earlier about moving in with you. With Justice gone and me always at your place, I feel someone else can use this spot." I explained to him.

Tony was excited that I was finally coming to his home permanently and assured me he will handle the sale of my condo; after all they did have a real estate company and this place would sell in no time with the view. We packed my clothes and other items and moved my things into his home that evening. Justice items were still there; but once the movers finished with my things, Tony had them remove her things and deliver them to her. So the condo was empty and we were both gone. The memories I had when I first moved in will forever be

with me. The fight with Kela started and ended here

as well as the nights Tony and I shared together. I

will never forget, this is where it all begin.

Chapter 8

It had been months since I heard from Justice and I was starting to worry. I had been calling her ever since the movers dropped her items off at her moms, but she was not answering her phone. So I decided to give her another call just to see what was up. "Hey Justice, what's up? I've been calling you for months now. Why haven't you been answering the phone?" I asked her. "Girl I haven't been answering the phone for anyone, Black is blowing my phone up day and night, I was afraid he would be right there with you and didn't want to deal in that drama. I don't know what I want to do, I mean I loved him but I think I am over it. So what's good?" Justice asked. I had to think about it for a while because she kinda' had my mind fucked up to think that I would call her with him standing next to me or in my presence. "Girl same old same old stuff, I sold the condo and now I am living with Tony, he thought it was for the best since Black had showed up at the crib after you told him. I did talk to Black, and I want you to know every time I called you I was alone. I wouldn't do that to you; but we heading to this club tonight called Anxious; it's a gentleman's club that they own. I wish I had you to roll with us, because you know how I feel going into these types of places solo. All them five dollars hoes gonna' be looking like I stole their man." I stated to Justice. "Girl I already know you going to go up in there and look like you own that muthafucker, I am not worried about you going as the only female because I know you can handle yours. But let me know how it goes and thanks for understanding my decision. I may decide to come to the place; I need to talk to Black. I feel like I need him to understand where I am coming from, and I kinda' miss him. You know how much I love to shop and love nice things, but I just feel that my life is not worth it. I will talk to you later okay gal." Justice said before hanging up. It was just morning and I knew I had a hundred things to do that day. I had to make sure my hair was on point, my make-up was to die for and my outfit was banging. I knew that meant I needed an appointment to get my hair pressed, my make-up applied and I had to get that perfect outfit. Since Tony was gone until later I decided to hit some of my favorite boutiques for that special gear. I had no idea where he could have went on a Saturday morning but I also knew this allowed me time alone to do what I do the best and that is to shop. I must have gone to ten different boutiques and still nothing that was interesting to me. I stopped at the last boutique and walked in. I was looking through the latest styles that the owner keeps aside for me when I notice that there were a couple of females looking and giggling my way. I just know these bitches ain't talking about me because I am the last one to fuck with. Then the owner told me not to worry about them they are just strippers who think they own the world. I then laughed and continued to look through the rack of clothes she had for me. I decided since I was going to a gentleman's club I should show a little more than usual. I picked out a short dress that was like a burnt orange color; this dress was cut down to the middle of my breast and was out in the back. I also found the perfect rainbow color shoes that were shimmering to perfection. I got some more items and told the boutique owner to put it on Tony's tab. That was what I was doing it now. Instead of purchasing my own clothes, Tony insisted that the stores I shop in create a tab that he can pay weekly. I walked right past those five dollar hoes and smiled. Dropped my Dolce shades over my eyes and I was out. Heading to the salon and then home.

When I arrived at the salon, it was packed. But I knew I was going to walk right in and get in the chair because my stylist knew I did not like to wait. The ladies were in here getting pretty for the club tonight talking about that guy they need to find to pay their way. I smiled knowing that I have already found my Mr. Right and he wasn't going anywhere. As long as I'm throwing this pussy at him left and right and having the perfect attitude, he was eating from the palm of my hand. Now don't get me wrong because the brother is packing twelve inches thick and he has a mean stroke with it. So I was eating from the palm of his hands as well.

I had already washed my hair so it didn't take long for me to get it pressed. I was in and out and my hair was flowing to perfection. It was silky just the way Tony liked it. When I got in the car my cell phone started to ring, it was my baby. "Hey baby, I just finished at the salon and I am on my way now to get dress." I told him. "That's cool, I was just checking cause I am home and I was looking forward to a little quickie before we leave." Tony stated while laughing. "Well you know it's whatever papi wants, I'm in route and I will see you in ten." I stated seductively. Traffic was backed up on Georgia 400 and now I was wishing I had taken the back streets. It took forty-five minutes longer to get home. When I got home Tony was not dressed and as he had said, he expected to get himself a little before we left. He didn't even give me enough time to get in the door before he grabbed me and placed me on the staircase. It was whenever and wherever when it came to sex with us, we were fucking like teenagers. He kissed me passionately as he always did and I just melted like ice cream. His kisses always made my pussy wet and I loved every moment of it. He took off my clothes and began sucking on my breast, one at a time and I was feeling the juices flow down my leg. Tony stuck his fingers in my pussy and whispered "I can see that you are ready for me, let me give you what you came for." And before I could reply he pulled out his manhood and he was ready to be showered with this waterfall. I straddled him and rode that horse all the way through the hills and the mountain. He turned me around and began fucking me from behind, I just loved this position and he knew it was my weakness. After about thirty minutes we both climaxed together.

"Baby that was nowhere near a quickie, the definition of a quickie is less than five minutes. If you wanted the full bar all you had to do was say so." I said to him with a big grin on my face. We took a shower together, laughed, and took the time to wash each other. After the shower, I was able to put on my outfit that I had purchased for the night. Tony was looking better than I was. He was dressed in a black button down Ralph Lauren shirt with the dark grey denim jeans to match. My man always looked his best when we went out and I loved him even more for that. I finally had a man that I did not have to dress. Tony looked at me and licked his lips before he said "damn baby that dress got my dick hard again, looks like we will be leaving the club earlier than I planned. A body like that needs all my attention." I smiled at him with my I know my body bagging look. I unwrapped my hair and we were ready to go. Tony had so many cars it was ridiculous, but he decided to take the four door Porsche tonight. The air was warm and we hit the streets.

When we got to the club it was packed outside, it's funny how men pay to come and see pussy that they see every weekend. I know people have to make their living some kind of way but I told myself this pussy has no price on it and I refuse to settle for less. With that being said that will be the reason why I have never stripped for money. Black was already in the club in the VIP section with a few more niggas and they had plenty of women in there with them. Tony grabbed a table in the far section of the VIP and we were sitting across from Black and the women he was paying. I can tell he was still hurting from Justice and was just trying to get over their situation. I talked to Justice earlier and she may be coming to the club to talk to him. She says she misses him and did not want me up in that club alone because bitches be tripping. But I'm not worried at all because I have a blade on my body somewhere. Many people will look at me and think I don't have anything on me but I have ways to attach blades to my body without anyone noticing. Tony was whispering in Blacks ear when I noticed this same bitch from the boutique earlier staring at us. I called Justice to see if she decided to come, "Hello, what's up girl?' she answered. "Nothing I was just checking to see if you decided to come, I'm sitting here with Tony and Black; but this bitch I seen earlier at the boutique is staring at me. They not paying the bitch any attention but I just feel like some shit bout to pop off." I explained to her while I still kept my eye on this bitch. "Girl you know, I wasn't gonna' let you be in that place alone, cause I know we have a lot of haters, I am actually outside parking the car, meet me at the door." Before I can hang up the phone, I told Tony I would be right back I am going to meet Justice at the door. Black must have heard me because he looked at me like what. And I walked off with that diva walk because I knew Tony eyes would be on me. As I was walking to the door I noticed the little ghetto bitch had grouped up with some more hoes and they all was staring at me. I was staring back because before those hoes thought they could get me I would have kicked they ass.

When I got to the door, I can see Justice walking up and I can say my cousin was looking just as good as I thought she would. She had on these five-inch silver shimmering wedge heels, some hooker black shorts and shimmering silver shirt with a short sleeve blazer over it. This bitch was to die for. Her outfit was off the chain and I was jealous for once in my life. I mean my cousin was looking greater than ever, she had them legs showing to perfection. All eyes were on her because she had a walk like a model on a fierce runway. I waved to the bouncer to let her in and I gave her a hug. "I'm glad you decided to come out and at least talk to Black, he misses you but you know how men are. They pretend not to care, when we know the truth. Now place your eyes on these bitches over here. The china doll black one is the one with the eye problem, she seems to have gained a crowd to encourage her." I told Justice softly. "Girl please that bitch can get it, it's whatever. I came because I already knew and I wanted to talk to Black, but let them hoes move I bet they won't be making it out this club tonight." Justice stated as she watched them bitches watch us. We made it to the VIP section and Black had made the strippers leave; and when they left the niggas that were with him left to. Black and Justice stared at each other for a while and then he stood up to face her. "You look beautiful tonight but you always looked beautiful to me." Black said right before hugging her. "Thanks, I just want you to know that I love you, I have for a long time. I was just a little shook up and I didn't know how to deal with it. I understand if you don't want to deal with me, but I hope we could at least be friends if you like." Justice explained looking all-professional in the face. Black was in shock by what she said then he responded, "Friends? Justice we are beyond friends, I want you to consider still being my lady cause I know you are a down ass chick. I see how your cousin rolls with my brother and I want the same thing. I want that ride or die and I want you to understand that I will never let anything happen to you, nothing and that's a promise." I was feeling so good at this moment because those two were back on point. We hung out and ordered bottles, danced and just enjoyed the night until these bitches decided to invade our private party.

The china black bitch spoke for the group "Yall niggas gonna pay for a dance or what? It's not often that we see y'all in here anymore. I guess we can see why now." This bitch had the nerve to interrupt and disrespect us. So I politely said "well since you see why they don't come in here anymore then get your two dollar ass out of here. These men here are well taken care of; you see a two-dollar hoe can't do anything for a million dollar man. So unless you want to see me whoop your ass, I will advise you to leave." Oh it was on from there, those bitches started running their mouths left and right. I jumped up, grabbed the china black bitch, and stuck my blade in her face and I said it again, "You either leave or wear my muthafucking name across your pretty little face.

I bet you won't make much money after that." She agreed and then they left. Tony and Black were laughing so hard. "Damn baby I didn't know you get gangsta like that, I was gonna handle them hoes but I see you had it under control. And Justice wasn't too far from you." Tony said with excitement. I looked at him and said "honey please, I take care of the bitches you handle them niggas. We do this for a living, hoes mess with us left and right when we go out because they're jealous." Black was laughing so hard when he said, "all I want to know is where the hell that blade come from? I mean no disrespect bro but she don't look like she carrying a blade on her. I would have never known." Justice was laughing before she said, "regardless of what we have on, we gonna either have a blade or a gun. It's hidden well with easy access." They just looked at each other like, do we need to worry. It was too funny. Tony decided he needed to go to the restroom, so he excused himself.

It had been about ten minutes and I noticed he still has not returned. I was wondering what the holdup was. Black and Justice was so wrapped up into each other that they haven't even noticed. "I'm going to the restroom and to check on Tony, I wanna' make sure he didn't fall in." I said laughing. On my way to the restroom, I hear Tony talking with this China bitch. What could they be talking about? I wondered. He never mentioned that he knew her when I was getting ready to slice her fucking face up. Now I am curious to know, so I ducked behind the wall where they could not see me. "Damn girl, why you have to be making a scene in front of my lady? I told you I don't want to have nothing else to do with you. What we did was in the past and now I am moving on, can't you see that." Tony whispered. "Well I would see that if you wouldn't be still paying my bills and buying my clothes and sending me money nigga. You met this bitch what a few months ago and now you have no time for me. It don't work like that, once you made a commitment to this pussy you in it for life. Niggas don't leave that easy. Tell me, if she your lady then why you still supporting me? Why you still coming to see me? Why you still calling me? Hell! Do you want me to ask you those questions in front of her?" China stated. I was in shock, I can't believe this nigga been playing me like this. Lacy don't get played for no man. Was my nose too wide open to see this? I just can't believe it. Then I heard Tony say "China, what we had was special and I did love you and I still have love for you, but my heart is no longer with you like that. The only reason I still support you is because of the way I walked out on you. I shouldn't have left like that, but I can't be your man if you're fucking all these other men. You would have had me looking like a fool in front of my brother and my business partners. Do you know the embarrassment you caused me when we went out on business matters? No you don't. I have to live with that shit. And the only reason why I still come and see you is to make sure you okay. We not fucking or cuddled up. It's business. Don't worry, you will not receive any more funds from me, cause I see now that you are making enough to support yourself." China started to put her arms around Tony and say in a low seductive voice, "Baby you know you still want to be with me, that chick you rolling with, she ain't your type. I know you like the mix breed but I really miss you." Tony removed her arms from his neck and was walking away when he turned around and said "I don't know if you noticed but that chick I'm rolling with is pure, I know her past and she knows mine, she may not know about you but tonight I intend to tell her. She is the realest woman I have ever been with and I intend to keep her by any means necessary. If you wanna fuck with her, I know she can handle you but I intend to handle you if you try to fuck with her in anyway. I no longer have time for your bullshit China. I will be sending you an eviction notice so I will advise you to find another place to live and if working in my club is going to cause any drama, you can find another establishment to shake your tired ass." I snickered to myself because this shit was too funny. That explains everything. I knew it was a reason this hoe was trying me. After Tony left, China went into the restroom. So I proceeded into the restroom and she looked stupid when she saw me. I stared at her and she stared at me, but I was not going to say anything about what I heard because I had to deal with him about this. China smacked her lips, applied her lipstick and walked out to hit the stage. Now don't get me wrong she was a bad bitch, but she was also a whore and I know a man like Tony need a woman that is going to be just for him. But I was going to deal with him later.

When I got back to our area Black and Justice was gone. Tony was talking to the waitress ordering some more drinks. "Hey, where did those two run off too?" I asked Tony. "They said they had some catching up to do and will catch up with us tomorrow if we want to have dinner or something." Tony said. Then he looked at me and asked, "where you been? You have been gone to the restroom a long time. I didn't see you on my way back." I looked him straight in the eye. "Yeah I know, I went looking for you but ran into something a little more interesting, so I decided I would just stand aside and see what your little meeting was about." I said with an attitude. He looked disturbed, because he knew at that moment, I had overheard the conversation with him and China. "Lacy, I know we have a lot we need to talk about, because I have not been quite honest with you, but let's not do this here." He stated. "Sure, no problem, let's not do this here. Let's just end this night now, I am ready to go! I feel stupid sitting here." I whispered. We got up; he left a tip for the waitress and proceeded to the car to head home. I knew he was not messing with her anymore but I just hate to be blind-sided with anything. I mean after all, I am the baddest chick walking in Atlanta and I know men come and go. But to think I have fallen in love with this man and moved in with him! I really let my guards down because my ass could not see nothing beyond the clouds. I got caught up and now I have to figure out a way out of this. I mean I love him, but I have to step back a few steps and regain myself. Strike one the family background, strike two the woman on the side and I don't think I can wait for strike three. I was quiet the whole ride home, just retracing my tracks and thinking where the hell did I go wrong. When we arrived at the house, I didn't even wait on Tony to open my door, he knew then I was pissed. We went inside and I went upstairs to get out of my clothes. It was late and I was not in the mood to discuss this mess tonight. "So, you're not going to talk about this tonight? You want to go to bed mad." Tony stated. "No I don't want to go to bed mad, but I also do not want to discuss this tonight if you don't mind." I said. "Lacy, it's not what you think, you heard everything so you should know that I am in love with you and I am not in love with her. I was only doing those things for her, because that's the type of man I am. She was not working when I left, so I didn't want to leave her on the streets or broke, she has a child. It's been about a year and that was my promise to her and she knew that. I didn't expect to find you and be in love before that year was up. To be honest, I thought I was not going to love again because that bitch really fucked me over. "Tony pleaded.

"Do you know how that makes me feel? No, you don't because you didn't care to at least warn me. I saw that chick in the store and I was wondering why she was looking at me and laughing. I am Lacy Pierce, I have to know what's going on around me. That was the only way I stayed on top of things. I have never walked into a situation without knowing it first. And here I am, jobless, homeless and backed into a corner. I gave up my life to be with you. I gave up everything because I loved you and I trusted you. Now I don't know what to do!" I said sobbing.

Tony looked me in my eyes and pleaded "You can continue to love me, and trust me. Believe me there is nothing with her or any other chick. I am a business man. I work and live to spend time with you. My father is back and I haven't even seen him as much because I want my time to be with you, Lacy I am sorry. You gave up everything for love, but you can still have it. If you feel you do not want to be with me for this reason I won't understand because I don't want you to go, but If I have too I will give it all back to you. I don't want you to feel like you have nothing. All of this is yours too. I don't put you on a budget, I let you spend what you want and if I have broken your heart I am sorry. If it's security you need in life, then first thing Monday morning we will go to the bank and I will withdraw one million dollars and put it in a bank account of your choice. Only you will have access to it. If we should ever split you will be set. I didn't do that for her I just simply paid her bills, but I am willing to do it for you because I see you are different and I trust you. Tony pleaded. I was in awe, I couldn't believe he was willing to do that for me. I was looking him in his eyes and thinking, maybe I was over reacting, and maybe I should give him another chance. "Tony you don't have to do that, the last thing I want you to think is I want your money. I just want you to be honest with me from here on out. Is there anything else I should know before we go to bed?" I asked. He looked at me and smiled. "Baby, there is nothing else I am keeping from you." He said. I was grateful for him, but I was still keeping my guards up, I can't let any more surprises come along. We kissed and hugged and cuddled for the night and went to sleep.

Chapter 9 (Tony)

I was laying in the bed with Lacy, but it was hard for me to sleep since I know the truth. I'm just laying here looking at the ceiling and thinking. It's hard lying to Lacy, but I know she's the one I want to spend eternity with. I don't know what to do. I love her with all my heart but if I tell her what's really going on with China I might lose her forever. Who am I kidding, I haven't even told my family the truth behind China. I think I will start with Black, maybe he will understand. I jump up, go into the bathroom and take a long shower. After I finish I puts on my clothes and get ready to head out for the day. "Good morning" lacy spoke. "Oh good morning to you baby, how did you sleep?" I asked. "I've had better nights, but I'm good." She responded. "I'm sorry to hear that you did not sleep that well but I'm sure your day will be better. I'm headed out to work so I will see you later. But you do what you do and enjoy your day. I will call you later." I explained to her. I gave her a kiss and went downstairs and out the garage door. I hated lying to Lacy, but I can't let her leave me. I have to come clean but what will the consequences be? While I raced to the office to wait for Black to arrive all kinds of thoughts were going through my mind. If China would just do what she has to do, I can be rid of her forever. It wouldn't be so bad if I wasn't still sleeping with her during the first two months of my relationship with Lacy.

Most women will understand, but Lacy, she's independent, beautiful and knows how to take care of herself. So she is not the type to sit around while a man who claims to be in a committed relationship with her cheats. I arrived at the office thirty minutes later and I see that Black was already here. Wonder why he is in the office so early? It's okay cause I can vent sooner than later now. I headed up the elevator to my office, shut off my out of the office voicemail and email. When I looked up Black was standing in the doorway. "Hey, what's up bro? I didn't expect to see you here this early." I stated "Yeah, a lots been going on and I wanted to get your opinion on some things with Justice." Black stated. "Well that's funny because I was looking to talk to you also about Lacy and I, so close the door and let's go." I responded. Black looked a little excited so I let him tell his information first, seemed like good news for him. While I waited, he pulled this small box out of his pocket. Was this what I think it is? Black placed the box on my desk and opened it; then he asked. "What do you think? I want to ask Justice to marry me. I had this ring custom made. As you can see its gold but it has ten karats." I was in shock, is this woman changing my brother? Of all the people I knew, Black was the last one I would think will get married. I guess it's time to change the game. "Damn Black, ten karats, that's deep. You must really love Justice! So when do you plan on proposing?" I asked "Well I was hoping to plan a trip to the Caribbean or Bahamas on the yacht. I also wanted you and Lacy to go to witness the proposal, so she would not expect anything." Black explained. "Well let's do it, we will fly to Miami get the yacht and head to the Bahamas. I will call Lacy to make sure she can go and you get Justice to go. We can leave in two weeks if you want." I told Black. "That's fine bro, so two weeks it is, I just know soon as we tell them they going shopping, cause they will swear they ain't got nothing to wear." Black said laughing. "So what is it that you want to talk to me about Tony?" Black asked.

"You know China right. Well it's more to it with her than what I have been saying. The only reason she has not told anyone or even Lacy is because we have an agreement and if she breaks the agreement it's over. This is hard for me and it was hard for me to keep it from my family. China and I have been married for some years now, her family is in China and it was against her culture to have a baby and not be married. After about a year of dating she found out that she was pregnant. I didn't want her to have an abortion because this is my child, at least that's what I thought, so we went to the courthouse and got married. We were planning to have a big wedding later after the baby was born. Well she had the baby, it was a little boy, but he was born was lung damages and died hours later in the hospital. I later found out that she had been using drugs during her pregnancy and this caused the baby to have failed lungs. I couldn't tell anyone about this because I felt so stupid. How could I have married a dope head, not knowing that she was using drugs? So when we got back home from the hospital, I beat her, I beat her so bad that she went back to the hospital, I almost killed her. I left her in the apartment on her death bed. Luckily she was able to call the police and get help. I was long gone, but she didn't tell the police who did it to her. She told them she was attacked while unlocking her apartment door and was beaten. She then came to me later after she recovered from the beaten and threatened me. I was so out of it that I didn't even take precautions to know that the bitch was recording our conversation. So I made a deal with her, I will pay her for the rest of her life, if she keeps this a secret and sign the divorce papers. We agreed but she has yet to sign the papers and now that she knows Lacy is in the picture, she is talking about telling Lacy and the police. She wants me to leave Lacy and be with her. Then I found out that the baby was not even mine, she had been sleeping around for months on me like I didn't mean shit to her. I'm just lost on what I should do." I explained to Black. He was looking in disbelief, and said "kill the bitch! And put her ass in the swamp somewhere. But how could you keep this from me bro, I thought we held no secrets from each other." I simply explained, "I was too embarrassed to let you know the truth, come on, you the roughest one of the both of us and I admire your strength, you think I can just tell my brother all this bullshit. It was hard. I actually look up to you believe it or not. You do things that I wish I can do. And what do you mean kill her?" I asked. Black sat down and started speaking, "Look bruh, if you think this dope headed bitch is just gonna walk away, you wrong! She set you up from the beginning with that baby shit. Then she comes to you after you damn near killed her wanting money but has not did what she had to do. Bruh all you have to do is say the word and her ass is gone the week we on vacation. I can set it up, because with her here you have a lot to lose but when she is gone nothing can get in your way. If you love Lacy and don't want to lose her I suggest you do what you need to do." I was thinking about what

Black was saying hard, I didn't want to be the cause of someone losing their life but at the same time my life is at stake here too. "Black I know that's why I love you, I wouldn't have asked for another brother, do what needs to be done and leave no evidence! I can't go forward with her in the way. But I need those divorce papers signed before it happens. What do you suggest be done about that?" I stated. "Give me the papers, I will take them to her now, that way you won't have nothing tying you to her ass when she comes up missing." Black responded.

I gave Black the papers and he walked out the office and went back to his own office. I was wondering if I am doing the right thing, hell at this point I got to do what I got to do, fuck the bullshit. This woman has been bringing me through the bullshit for years and until I found Lacy, I didn't realize what was happening. I just hope Black makes sure she is never found. Nobody is going to miss her ass, her family in China and she just got junkie friends here. I am finally getting my life back and can move the fuck on with Lacy. By the way let me call her and let her know about this trip we taking in a few weeks. "Hey babe!" Lacy said when she picked up the other end. "Well hello beautiful, I wanted to let you in on a few things, but only if you can keep a secret." I told her. She laughed and said, "What you mean if I can keep a secret? I've been holding on to your secret for over a year now. So what you got for me?" I smiled because I knew she was my ride and die chick, Lacy has drove the car when I popped a few niggas and picked up a few shipments for me when I couldn't make it. She is the truth and I would be lost without her. "Well Black came to me this morning with an offer to go to the Caribbean or Bahamas with him and Justice. He wants us all to fly to Miami and take the yacht to one of the islands. But to top it off, he is proposing to Justice and she has no clue. He's in love and I am happy for him and he wants us to be a part of it. Now he is only telling her we taking a vacation, so I need you to not mention it to her, I mean the proposal." Lacy was screaming and excited in the phone before she said. "Tony now that's a secret I can keep, I am so happy for them. And we are going to have a ball on the island. I just hope they can handle that. So it's settled! Let me get out of this bed and get my day started, love you babe and I will talk to you later!" Okay, Love you too!" I sealed the phone called and told Black the news.

Chapter 10 (Black)

Out of all people, I can't believe the shit my brother just told me, never the less kept from me. Hell we family and family as tight as us holds no secrets. I was in shock standing there in his office as he gave me the run down on old girl. I knew she was a base head from the beginning but who you love at the time is who your love and flaws are overlooked. I already know what I have to do. And since I have the divorce papers in my hand she will sign them today or else and I am going to make sure she signs them. Let me call the club and see if her ass is working. This way I can have her sign them in front of a crowd and when she comes up missing, we won't be suspected. I called the club and Red answered the phone, I was happy it was him that answered cause he keeps it one hundred. "Ah Red this Black did China come in to work yet?" I asked him. He was speaking like he was getting his dick sucked, "H-e-y w-h-a-t-s u-p B-la-c-k? I saw her c-o-m-e in earlier and she set to be here till midnight." Red said stuttering in the phone. I just told him, "good I will be there in a few and nigga take that shit like a man quit stuttering on the muthafucking phone." And I hung up the phone. I had to get over to the club offer this bitch some dope and have her sign. I know she is going to accept it because she is a dope head. Everybody knows once a dope head always a dope head.

I know Tony is going to be in them boring ass meeting all day so he won't miss me for a few hours. I hate meetings and that's why I handle the gangster part of the business and he handles the business part. I have to maintain the dope supply and make sure it's being push from overseas to our location. See that was a little information that we kept from the ladies. The less they know the better. Tony comes in and cover the trail of money by investing in businesses and tampering with the books so it will look like that company made the money. Boy if Justice and Lacy really knew our hustle they probably leave us but then again they can see. I put my do not disturb sign on the door and went out the back way. I didn't want anyone to come bothering me or know that I had slipped out. There were no cameras in the building where we work except the entrance and exits that the public or employees used. We know having a surveillance system can incriminate you so we chose to do without it and we have a personal door that leads to our personal parking and no cameras in the area. I used the personal elevator that only me and my brother have access to and went to my car.

Traffic in Atlanta was crazy and I had to make sure I made it to the club and back within a few hours. I jumped in my Ford six fifty and speed off. I loved this truck because it sits up high and I got it raised with them country ass white boy tires on it.

Traffic seemed okay since morning rush hour was gone; it was not going to be long before people start getting off work. I made it to the club in no time. The parking lot was pretty full; it was always men from their office coming in on break and lunch to get them a dance so their wives wouldn't know. That's why we picked this spot because no matter what a man wants to see some pussy other than his wives.

I walked in the club and went to the office; Red was sitting in there with a grin on his face. He must have finished getting his school kid blow job. "Ah nigga, what bitch had you stuttering on the phone? You need to learn how to control that shit and ram that bitch throat with your dick and she will be moaning." I said to him laughing. "Oh it was some new chick trying to get a job here, I told her I may consider her and to let me see what she working with, but I also told her that was not part of the job nigga! And I can hold mines I just tried to sound professional on the phone with you." Red explained. I can tell this nigga was new to the pussy because a nigga got to control the pussy the pussy don't control the nigga. I had Red go and get China a few more girls and to bring her back to me. I had a plan that was a sure way to get her to sign the document. If she simply didn't know what she was signing she was good. While waiting on them my phone rung and it was Justice. "Hey, what's up baby?" I asked. She was a breath of fresh air on the phone. "Hey Black, I was checking to see what time we going to dinner tonight? I was going over my moms and just wanted to make sure I'm back in time to freshen up." Justice asked. "We can go around nine or ten, whatever you like, just be careful. Alright! Talk to you later." I said and hung up. Justice and I never really said I love you at the end of our conversations like Tony and Lacy; we just keep it simple because she knows my heart and I know her heart. No sooner than I hung up Red came back in with these thirsty hoes. They was looking at me like I said come give me a dance. I told them to take a seat and I then I said "I know you all are wondering why you are here. Well we have to make sure we keep everyone's trust and loyalty to the club. I have come up with some contracts that tell us you are willing to commit yourself to this club for at least six months before leaving. I just need you to sign the back page and date it and have the person next to you sign as a witness. And then you may go." At first when I mentioned loyalty China was looking at me like she was scared. Yeah I know bitch that you ain't loyal, but soon you will be broke too. She signed it, had the lady on the side of her sign and passed the paper to me once she was finished. I'm glad the signature page on the divorce papers didn't have anything on there about divorce, just the basic for signing. After everyone signed the papers and left my office, I made sure that I kept China's papers and placed them behind the divorce order. Now all I had to do was stop by the notary and have her notarize it. She will do it without China being present, hell she works in my office she has no choice. That is why we got her the notary stuff in the first place. All was left was to set that bitch up and have her dead before our vacation. I know I told my brother when we on vacation, but it's better this way so he won't know who did it. I can make him think I didn't have anything to do with it so it will be free from his thoughts. I left the club and headed back to the office, traffic again was not bad at all. Right before I got to the office Red called me and said there was a problem with China. She was acting crazy like she was on crack. I turned around because I knew Red did not know China smoked crack. But that gave me the opportunity to give her this bad crack I have. That was my plan but I did not want anyone to see me give it to her. Once I pulled back in the club I can tell China was phening for a hit. I asked her to come in my office and acted real professional with her so people can see. Once we got inside I talked to her and told her I had something to fix this mess. She was excited like a child in a candy store. I gave her the bad crack and told her to leave the club if she is going to be smoking that shit. And act like everything is cool. She did as I told her, gathered her stuff. She told Red she wasn't feeling well and will be back in the morning. And China left! I was glad cause within a few minutes where ever she smoke that crack is the last place she will be seen. I was hoping she will go home and smoke it and someone will find her soon and declare she had some bad crack. But knowing China, she's ready to smoke now so she will find a crack house around the way. When I left I didn't see China anywhere in sight, just hope she get it over with and soon. I finally made it back to the office and was able to sneak back in my office just in time. Soon as I sat down, Tony knocked on the door. All his problems will be over soon. "What's good bro? I'm finish with all these meeting. I called Lacy too and told her about the trip so we in." Tony said. I can tell he was still thinking about that shit with China. I placed the envelope on the table and told him to get it filed as soon as possible. "I went to the club, brought a few more ladies in with China and asked them to sign a contract, at least that's what they thought they were signing. Then I had them witness each other's contract. China signed this divorce paper. So congrats, you are now a free man." I said before getting up and hugging him. I can tell my brother was excited about this, now he's free. He looked at me and said. "So this means, you don't have to kill her now right." If he only knew the killing was already in motion. That's why I did it the way I did because I want him to think it was the drugs. "Yeah it's cool, she's still alive and you have your divorce bro, don't worry about it." I explained. Tony left for the day and I was following his path. I had a lot of products to inspect and I still planned on going out with Justice, so I needed to do what had to be done.

Chapter 11

I can't believe that Black is ready to propose to Justice, I mean just a few months ago she wasn't even talking to him. But he must really love her and I am so happy for them. But I still have this issue with Tony, I don't know what's going on with him and this china bitch, but I am going to find out sooner than later. I have my girls to help me with a little investigating. See I don't let my friend meet my men or my men meet my friends, it's too complicated and if I ever need to set him up, the men will never know that this sexy ass bitch sitting in front of them is a personal associate of mines. I am meeting one of my dearest friends today, because I know if I want this done right she is the one that can do it. I need her to get the inside scoop from China herself cause bitches talk when they think someone is interested.

I decided since it was a cool sunny day I will wear my white linen pants with a sheer blouse and my bra underneath. I was meeting her downtown Atlanta at Décor Seafood and Sushi. It was a classy spot so I had to dress the part and besides my girl will be even hotter because once again I only roll with the hottest, sexiest bitches around. I jump in the shower and washed my hair because I needed to wear it natural today. Once I was finish with my hair and getting dressed, I made it out the house just in time. I was to meet Bria in forty-five minutes and she hates it when people are not on time.

Traffic was light and so I made it in thirty minutes. I valet parked my car and headed inside, requested a table in the rear out of sight just to be sure that Tony did not know my game. When I arrived Bria was not there yet, I went ahead and ordered two champagnes because I knew she was probably valet parking her car at this point now. And I was right, in walks Bria five foot eight, dark skinned diva. Her complexion was to die for. I always wanted to be a darker tone after meeting her and all the men would fall to her feet. Her body was banging, she was petite in the waste with a donkey ass and hips that complimented her frame. She was gorgeous and a jack of all trades.

"Hey girl, long time no see, and I see you looking beautiful!" I said while extending my arms to give my bestie a big hug. She smiled and while hugging me said. "Oh I miss you so much, Lacy! You just don't understand. I miss those clubbing nights where we made the men drool and the women mad." We took our seats and began catching up on old times and new ones that we have missed. Bria knows I only wanted to see her to fulfill a job because this is what we did for each other. If she needs me I am there and when I need her she is there, it's for our own protection that we are never seen together again. Bria began speaking, "So what's this job that you want me to do? I would like to know what the task will be?" I sighed and began, "Well I have been dating this guy for awhile now, a baller I mean real money baller. He's a twin but Justice and I met them in the club and we started dating, she's dating the brother. You know I have my own money but he has the money. He has me set up at different stores to charge it to his account and he never questions what I spend or how much. He has bought me a car not just any car but the most expensive car a girl could ask for. But some months later I ran into this broad at one of the boutiques I shop at on him, getting clothes to go out for the night because they own this strip club. Bitch was in there talking reckless, looking at me and giggling, I paid the broads no mine because they looked like a bunch a junkies to me. But later that night in the club, I seen the same bitch and that's how she knew who I was because she worked there and was an employee of the twins. Well I overheard parts of a conversation with her and Tony,

I only heard the part where he told her he was finished with her and she needs to do what she needs to do about some documents. He presented it to me like it was only business, he admitted to being with her years ago but I believe it's some shit that he can't get swept under the rug. I need you to go in as one of the baddest bitches around and land a job as a stripper. I'm sure she will relate to you because at work she is a completely different person. Don't get me wrong she looks like she a drug head but she is beautiful. And you know how women talk when the enemy is in the building. I plan on being in the building with him this weekend, but auditions for new dancers is tomorrow. Do you think you can do this for me?" Bria was looking at me for a while before she spoke. "Damn girl sounds like you hit the jackpot! I'm happy that you found someone to spoil you like you need to be. But do you think it's good to open up that closet of skeletons? I mean what if I find out something that you don't want to accept. You can't undo what was done. I am down with doing it and I have my gear in the car but I want to be sure that this is what you want. Because what I see in your eyes that I have not seen in a while is love and hurt. You love him! But the information can break or make this relationship. So you just make sure, but I am here to help at any means and I want you to know the truth."

I gave Bria the package and of course I am paying my girl, that's what we do. She has everything she needs and I am sure she will get the job. We talked and finished eating and said our good byes in the distant. I let Bria leave first and ten minutes later I exited the restaurant as well. Right on time! Because soon as I got in the car Tony called me. "Hey babe, what's up?" I asked. " Hey, I'm heading home in a hour, did you want to make plans for dinner or just have the chef cook up something at home?" he asked me. "Let's eat in, I will call the chef and have something special prepared for us tonight, so I will see you when you get home sweetie, Love you!" I stated. "Cool" he said and hung up the phone. I called the chef and told him what needed to be prepared tonight and I headed home to get ready for what was going to happen. I needed to clear my thoughts and act normal with Tony, I know he feels like I know something. But today on the phone he sounds better than ever like a burden has been lifted off his shoulders. I will know sooner than I think all I need to know and this will be the make or break moment.

Dinner was great and things with my baby seemed better than ever. We talked in front of the fireplace for hours and then he held me and we dosed off right there like lovers do. I can't remember the last time I have felt this good with a man. But now I have to find out the truth even if it hurts me, I have to know what I am in for. This will be the moment to make or break this relationship. Bria is a sure fit for the club and I know she will be selected as one of the new dancers, with me and Justice as interviewers, I know she is in. Of course Tony and Black will be there as well. This morning seems strange to me, I have a feeling something is not right but I guess I will let life take its course. Tony and I arrived at the club before Justice and Black. I can see the potential ladies lined up in front of the club. Everyone knows that auditions at this club are on a first come first serve basis, but only for the finest and prettiest in Atlanta. Tony cleared his throat after seeing all the ladies and said "damn, the ladies are hot today!" I looked at him and smirked before I said "better watch it, I'm the only hot lady in your life." We both burst out laughing. I knew he was just trying to make me jealous but I already know his type and a stripper ain't one of them. That's why I can't seem to put my hand on this China chick. Justice and Black pulled up and then we all exited the vehicles. The ladies were putting on their best show when they saw the twins. The twins have been the hottest thing in Atlanta for years and women will throw themselves at them at any chance they get. Justice and I didn't mind because we know that we are two of the baddest bitches around and you had to have a lot to fill our shoes. We did the usual, which was Tony and Black unlock the club go in and set up and while they did that Justice and I picked ten ladies each to start the auditions. Most women knew before they left if they have the job and others were called later that day. It wasn't hard for me to spot Bria because she was one of the first five ladies in line. I immediately started from the front and picked her second to this Asian chick. Once we were finished picking we headed in the club and started the auditions. The ladies had their choice of song and needed to be ready when their name was called. Compared to Bria I made sure that the other ladies could not top her in beauty or sexiness. So let the auditions begin. The club needed ten additional ladies and there had to be about one hundred outside waiting.

The first up to dance was the Asian black chick that I picked, she had a nice petite shape but we knew the men in this club liked to see ass and titties and not those itty-bitty things that most women have. This chick has big tits but no ass. She never stripped before and we can tell. Next few ladies were okay but here comes the prize that I have been waiting on. Bria came out with a white nurse uniform on, some red knee high stockings her g-string beneath and some pumps that will kill a nigga. Her song choice was Luke, and we know he was nasty. Once the music started Bria did her thang, she popped her ass every way possible, stripped and did seductive moves. I know she was a keeper. After the auditions the ladies were mingling in the club. Tony and Black went in the office to pick the ones they want to hire based off their scores. I knew Bria was a sure fit. I made it my business to mingle with the ladies introducing myself to the ones I know made it. "Damn girl, you put in work up there on that stage! If I was a nigga I would have scooped you up." I said to Bria as I was walking up on her. She pretended like she didn't know me and said, "Thanks girl, I just hope I was good enough to get the job. I was nervous!" Bria was really playing the part and that's what I love about her, no matter the situation she knows to stay in role until the task is complete. "Well, we will be seeing a lot of you around here because I know you are in, you were one of the best we had." I said to her before walking off. As I was making my way back to the office, Tony and Black came out to get all the ladies that they have selected to represent at the club! Out of the ten they selected, Bria was a sure in, she was the first name they called and I knew my plan was in action. All I had to do was sit back and wait for shit to unfold.

It's been a week and Bria has been working the club day and night. She was paid well from me but she was paid even better at the club. Once niggas got word of the new chick with the banging body they came from miles just to see her sex appeal. Most of her time was spent doing private dances in the VIP. She was bringing home five grand a night, damn maybe I should have applied for one of the dancer spots but I know Tony would not be hearing that. I met Bria at our local spot to get any information that she may have gotten from China. "Hey girl, so what's the word? Have you been able to get any information out of the bitch?" Lacy asked. Bria sighed and said, "Girl I'm tired as hell working up in that club day and night and this bitch haven't even been there. I overheard some girls talking about how she got in some trouble and how they have been by her spot and no answer. I believe something has happened to her cause no one has seen her or even heard from her. Maybe it's for the best." Damn, I thought to myself, where could this bitch be? She is the only one that can give me the information I need since Tony thinks he can only tell me part of the story.

I looked at Bria and gave her a smirk before I said. "Well I guess it's for the best, but I was for certain that I will find out what they are hiding before we head to the island. But I guess I will be waiting till I get back and find out, but I wonder where she could be, maybe her ass is in jail. Bria thank you so much for doing this for me and I have the rest of your money right here. I guess I will see you next time I need a favor. Man I wish I can see you every day but I know it's too dangerous for us to be seen together since we've done so much bull shit in the past. I love you girl and I will let you know if something happens." We hugged and Bria said, "girl please you don't have to give me that money, I took the first payment and after making over forty thousand dollars this week, I don't need it. I didn't know that club was jumping like that so I know your nigga paid, mad paid. But I will miss you too and I love you, until next time." She walked off and Bria was gone again for a few more years. Tony and Black are going be disappointed that their star money maker won't be showing up again. Oh well, now I have to finish packing because we will be leaving soon for this vacation and surprise proposal. I decided to hit up Lennox mall since I was right around the corner to finish up some shopping for the trip. The mall is not packed during the week and I enjoy going to all my favorite spots without having to wait in line or wait for help. I was in and out and now it was time to head home. While riding up four hundred, wondering where could this chick be at? I needed that information and now she MIA. I love Tony but I know he's hiding something from me, I just know it. I have always been the type to say don't go snooping for things because what happens in the dark will come to light. That's why I have never followed a nigga, looked through his phone or even questioned where he has been in the late night because it shows up right on time. I mean all the information you need comes to the light all the time. So what was different about this situation? Was it the fact that I knew who this bitch was and I knew it could be more? I'm just going to leave it alone and enjoy the time I have with this man. If it is more to it then it will come to the light. I was so into my thoughts that I did not hear my phone ring as many times as it did. Justice had called me three times, damn I was thinking hard. And now she's calling again. "Hey girl, my bad I was in deep thought, you know how I get." I explained in the phone. Justice was breathing a little hard and said. "Girl get your ass down to the jail now, they just arrested Black and Tony at the club. I was on the phone with Black when the police raided the place. I heard the noise and all I heard him say was call Lacy and come bail us out and the line disconnected. I went to the club but everyone was gone and the club was being searched by the Feds." I was in shock, what could be the problem? "Girl where are you I am on my way, I can't believe this shit. I wonder why the club was raided and by the Feds at that." I yelled in the phone at Justice. Justice responded, "I'm at Black's house so I will see you when you get here and hurry." We hung up the phone and I found myself doing one ten in my new four door Porsche that Tony bought me. Good thing Black lived around the corner from us, because I was only about ten minutes away but at the speed I'm going I made it in five. Justice didn't give me time to get out the car. She came running out the house and jumped right in. I pulled off and we were heading downtown to the Russell Building to see why Tony and Black were taken in custody. See Justice was thinking jail, but when the Feds pick you up, you go straight to the federal building for interrogation and they have a jail inside also. "Do you know why they were arrested? Did Black say anything else to you over the phone?" I asked Justice to see what else she may know. Justice looked at me and I can tell she was trying to remember something but instead she said, "Nothing, I have no idea what they were arrested for. I was trying to figure that out myself. Since being with Black all I could think about is that they either killed someone, had someone killed or one of them little hustlers snitched on them." I had to admit, the twins do a lot of undercover shit and this little life may have just come to an end. But I am here to hold my man down and I know Justice is going to hold her man down. We rode the rest of the way in silence, I was thinking of anything that may have happened.

Chapter 12

We arrived at the Russell Building thirty minutes later, only to be given the run around by this fat bitch that calls herself security at the front door. We were told to have a seat and someone will be with us when they can. It's like we sat there forever waiting on someone to give us information on the twins. After about two hours of waiting this tall white FBI agent came out and greeted us. He apologized for the wait and escorted us back to his office. Then he spoke, "The two gentlemen that you ladies are here to get are not being released at this time, we are holding them for further questioning on a missing person possible murder case. We have evidence that these men may have been last seen with our informant. She was getting ready to get the final piece of evidence that we need and now she has disappeared. Have any one of you ever met China, she worked at the club and has been missing for a week now?" I was in shock about what he was saying, because this bitch was working there and snitching at the same time. I can't believe their holding them for this bitch. I was looking at the agent with hate in my eyes. I spoke softly yet spicy, "I don't know what type of games you people are playing but they have nothing to do with a missing possible dead person, especially not this China bitch. She probably somewhere tricking off cause that's what she do the most. She worked at the club and because she works there, they are suspects. Seeing that you said missing person, there should not be a murder charge because you have no body. Let's see that hold up in court. You better have enough proof to just hold them here like this and why haven't they received a phone call yet?"

The agent was looking at me like I was crazy but he said. "Are you aware of China's relationship with Tony? You obviously don't know their history now do you? He was engaged to her and they got married, he beat her and left her to die when he found out that she lost their child. She was a drug addict because she got addicted after dating him and it was her fault that the baby died and he blamed her for it. He's still married to her, he's been paying her to keep it a secret and to sign the divorce papers but she has not signed those papers yet. She told us who did this to her and we made a deal with her. We told her to make him think that she didn't tell who done it and blackmail him. Get back in good with him so we could get the inside on their operation. We were getting all that we needed from her but when you came in the picture, he stop dealing with her and it put our investigation on hold. But now as we are getting ready to move in, our key witness disappears." I was in shock I can't believe that this nigga is married to this snitch ass bitch. I can't believe he's been fooling me all this time. I am such a fool but I won't be a fool any further. I don't wish any bad on anyone and I hope I find that bitch before they do because I am going to whoop her ass just like Tony did. My phone rung and I answered it quickly because I did not recognize the number, "Hello, I said in my soft voice trying to keep myself from getting pissed. "Lacy, thank god you answered, I'm at the Russell Building with Black, we've been arrested on some bullshit about China being missing or possible dead. I need you to call my attorney and have them meet us here to get us bail because they have no proof or evidence." Tony said. I responded calmly, "Yeah baby, I know. Justice and I are here now but I will call the attorney and have them meet us here. See you soon." And I hung up the phone. I turned to the FBI agent and said. "Well I am sure you know that was them and now we have to get going. However, before I go, I need to know, are you going release them now since you have no evidence or proof, or do

I really need to call the lawyer and have them released and then slap your department with a suit for bullshit." He looked at me with shock in his eyes because he knew I was telling the truth and he knew he had nothing on them so they have to let them go. "Save your phone call, they will be released within the next few minutes, you ladies can have a seat back in the waiting room and they will be out shortly." He stated.

Justice and I walked back in the waiting room and from the way she was looking at me I can tell she wanted to know if I was okay. So before she could say anything, I said "I'm okay! I knew something was going on but I didn't have any proof but I guess I got the truth today." Justice responded, "Girl I know you're going to be fine cause that bullshit he just fed you can't keep you down, so what are you going to do?" I looked out the window and said, "I am going to confront him when we get home. I'm not going to make a scene in front of you and Black, I will talk to him alone. Besides she seems to be out the picture now." We both looked at each other and started laughing. I was thinking wherever this bitch is she can stay there. I had to make myself forget about what I just found out until I get home then I was going to question his ass in a very mature manner. It took another five minutes and Black and Tony was walking out the door. They looked at us and came walking up, we hugged and headed out the door to my car. Everyone was silent during the whole ride. I dropped Black and Justice off at his home and me and Tony headed to his house, which was right around the corner. Once we entered the garage, he went upstairs ran back downstairs and locked his office door while making phone calls. He must suspect something is wrong with me because he can't even look at me in my eye. It was all too funny to me. I dismissed the staff for the evening and told them to come back in the morning. After letting them out, I set the alarm and went to Tony's office. Knock, knock, knock. "Yeah!" he screamed through the door. "Hey it's me, I let the staff go home. We need to talk for a minute?" I told him. It took a few seconds and then the door open, he was standing there looking all sexy in his suit. I walked in, left the door open and sat down. He walked back over to his desk and took a seat. He looked me in the eye for the first time since we left the station and I remembered why I loved him so much. How could this man that I love so much be lying to me? I was lost for words but I knew he knew I knew his secret. I exhaled and begin talking, "I didn't call the lawyer because we were actually talking to the head agent when you called me, so I just told him since he had no evidence or proof he needed to let you go before I call the attorney and have them sued. So you may want to call and give your attorney the heads up on your recent arrest. I was also told the reason you were there and I want to know if it's true?" "Is what true?" he asked. "Is it true that you are married to that bitch China that I questioned you about? And who you damn near beat to death because she was the reason your child was born with a hole in the lung. Were you going to tell me any of this? And how you've been paying her because you thought she wasn't going to tell the law and give you a divorce. Hell she's working for the law, she's their informant. She told on your ass that night and they have been following your operation since then. So whatever she has told, now she's missing or even dead they say. I just want to know how could you hurt me like this? I am so in love with you and I didn't think you would ever lie to me. I expect it from your business because I don't want to know about that but this, this is just too much." I said with tears falling from my eyes. Tony could do nothing but put his head down before speaking, he couldn't bear to look at me like this. "Baby I know it must hurt finding out this way, but the truth is, I didn't want to lose you and I don't want to lose you now. Yeah I was married to her and I still am but I haven't messed with her in years. Way before you and I met, I had been trying to get her to sign the divorce papers but now that she knows about us she continues to refuse. Black was able to get her to sign them the other day and I filed them immediately. I have not seen her or touched her and I have no idea where she is. And I am not worried about them using her as an informant because she knows nothing about my business, nothing at all. And that's why they couldn't keep us. But I don't want to lose you. Please tell me you are not going anywhere because what we have is special and I need you in my life."

It's like I am not sure of what I want to do, I love this man and at the same time I can't and won't be anybody's fool. I came into this relationship giving it all I can and I have just been slapped in the face from a bitch that I don't even know. "Tony, you know I love you and it's a lot to digest. But what would it have hurt if you would have told me this information from the beginning. I wish you would have given me the opportunity to know if I wanted to be with you or not. It's like you took my choices away by leaving out this information. How do I know you didn't have anything to do with her disappearing and I how do I know you won't try to make me disappear? I don't know! What do you expect me to do? I can't be a fool, I am most certainly a fool in love. But you know what they say fool me once shame on you fool me twice shame on me! I really have to think about this. Once we come back from the trip, I hope to have an understanding. I'm still going because I am going to support my cousin and I want to be there for that special moment but until then I will be staying elsewhere." I said with hurt in my voice. I didn't even give Tony time to respond, I left his office went upstairs and packed me a few bags and I left.

Chapter 13 (Justice)

It was the day of the trip and I didn't even know if Lacy was coming. The last time I spoke with her was the night we picked up the men from the federal building and she was so upset. She told me she was still coming and that she will see me today but she haven't answered her phone in a few days. Tony haven't heard from her and I was starting to get concerned. Out flight leaves in a couple of hours and we are almost at the airport now. I was riding with Black and we picked up Tony. While I'm daydreaming and looking out the window I hear Tony and Black talking. "Man I really fucked up, I should have just told her from the beginning and went from there." Tony stated. "Ah bro, you did what you felt you needed to do, China is the past and Lacy is the future. I think she will look at the circumstances and give it a try. She has to know where your heart is." Black said.

We arrived at the airport and checked our bags in, still no sign of Lacy. I tried calling her again but she still didn't pick up. Once we arrived at the concourse after about forty five minutes of security, we were ready to take this flight. I can tell Tony was feeling down but I know everyone will make the best of the trip. We all standing and looking out the window when we heard Lacy say, "It's about time you guys got here, I've been waiting and drinking. I thought I was going to be taking this flight alone." We turned around and I gave Lacy a big hug, Tony gave her a hug and Black. I said "Girl we thought you wasn't going to make it. I was calling you and calling you to see if you wanted to ride with us and no answer." Lacy looked at me and then went to her purse and grabbed her phone before saying, "girl my damn phone is messed up and I just haven't had time to go get a new one, so I said fuck it I will get one when I come back. I'm not going to be able to use it anyway while we're on the yacht." We laughed and I told the men that we will be back. Lacy and I talked and she assured me that she was okay. She was going to make the best out this trip and have fun. She just needed to get some space with all that was introduced to us that day. We boarded the plane and sat in first class like we booked. Black and I were seated next to each other, Lacy and Tony was seated next to each other. I could see he was making small talk with her and I hope they get it together soon. We took off, Miami here we come. I looked at Black and he was knocked out before the plane could take off. He was a mess but I loved him. I can't wait till we get back to tell him the news. I left Black but later discovered that I was pregnant. When I came back, I didn't want to tell him without being sure. But yesterday it was confirmed from my doctor that I am two months pregnant. Besides I have to tell him soon before I start showing. I know Lacy may be happy for me because it's a baby, then again she may be sad because we won't be hanging like we used too. I 'm sure she will understand. I glanced out the window at the clouds. They were always so beautiful from the sky, look like fluffy cotton. It's amazing how things are created and we should enjoy them every day. Our flight was only an hour and thirty minutes, we landed in Miami but had to wait because they had to clear an area for us to exit. It was like forever, I was ready to get this vacation started. Since we didn't board the yacht until tomorrow morning, we all had agreed to take over Miami tonight and party. But there will be no drinking for me. We were finally able to exit and headed towards baggage claim. We all retrieved our bags and the guys already had limo service waiting for us at the curb. It wasn't the average limo, it was one of those Mercedes Sprinter Vans that the celebrities ride around in. It was very spacious and we did not have to drive. On the way to the hotel I could see Lacy and Tony were really talking things through. I couldn't hear their conversation but I hoped it was for the good. I know one thing we better stop and get something to eat soon, this baby is hungry. I looked at Black and caught him looking at me, I didn't realize that I had been rubbing my stomach. I hope he don't suspect anything. "Why you rubbing your stomach?" he asked me. I looked startled and said, "Huh, oh I'm just hungry, I haven't eaten since last night. Are we going to stop and get something to eat soon?" Black was looking at me like something ain't right but I knew the coast was clear when he said, "yeah baby, we're just going to check in the hotel and go grab lunch at one of these restaurants. Can you hold on a few more minutes? Or do we need to stop at Micky Dee's?" Black was always cracking jokes but this one wasn't funny. "Yeah that's cool." I said to ease my tension. Damn, how far is the damn hotel away.

They said we were staying at one close to the dock so that we can be ready to board tomorrow. They had everything all set up. They had the staff prepared to sail with us, the food, the chefs and entertainment. I heard the boat was like a house floating on water and it will be more than enough room. Just get me there and get me some food. I hope I don't get sea sick while I'm pregnant. I am already vomiting every morning till about noon during the day.

Chapter 14 (Lacy)

The flight was great, Tony and I talked the whole time and it was refreshing to hear what he's been doing. Of course he wants to know where I am staying. Do I have enough money? Where we stand? And when am I coming home? I tell you he didn't waste no time with this. I would think he would have got the point when I didn't return his phone calls or text messages. But I have to say this man is looking awfully sexy and I knew if I would have agreed to meet him I would have forgotten the reason I was mad at him in the first place. I know my heart and my heart loves him but I am not telling him until we get back that I will come back home. I mean look at the situation, this was before me and all he tried to do was protect me because he loved me. That's what men are supposed to do, to protect you from being hurt if they love you. I figured it would be me and him getting married first but I guess he has another plan. Sitting next to him on the plan I was trying my best to keep my composure because he was wearing my favorite cologne and smelled so delicious and it's not easy sitting in this damn van with him. I am going to fuck the hell out of him tonight just to show him that I am and will always be all he needs in a woman. "So Lacy, you know this trip is all about you and Justice and whatever you ladies want you shall have. Just say the word." Tony whispered in my ear. And why the fuck he do that, got my ass all hot from his smooth sexy breathe on my ear and neck. Damn a bitch got to hold it together. "You know we will, it's not a problem! But thanks." I replied in my sexy voice. He was ready now, I can tell he kept putting his hand between his legs to keep his dick from popping up that leg because he was horny as hell. It was too funny to me. We arrived at the Alliance Hotel and checked in. Tony and Black had packages delivered to the hotel and they were waiting for them when we arrived. I wonder what they had ordered to be shipped here. We all went up to the presidential suite which was a combination on 3 large luxury bedrooms, a large luxury den, kitchen and large bathrooms. Once we got into the room, Tony and I picked our room and Justice and Black went to their room.

I was curious to know what was in the box, so while I was unpacking I asked. "You guys had packages delivered here, what's in the box?" Tony looked at me like I asked him a trick question. "We had these boxes shipped because we could not carry these guns on the plane and did not want to chance them being removed from our suitcases. Just the necessity to stay protected." Tony explained. I forgot they can't carry guns on the plane and these niggas carry guns everywhere they go, but I assumed since this was a special occasion and a vacation they will leave the bullshit behind. Once I finished putting my items in the closet I decided to take a shower before we head out for something to eat. I needed to get out of my flying suit and into something a little sexier that will have Tony drooling and aching for this pussy. I decided to show my legs on this beautiful day, so I picked out a pair of navy blue shorts and a navy blue and white striped shirt that was missing the back. It had a collar and only two straps to keep the sides from flying up. This was an Alberta Ferretti designer special that I could not pass up.

I just love her clothes. They are expensive but I got to have them. I went on into the bathroom and it was so amazing, the shower was huge and there were four shower heads from different sides of the shower. I guess I will be wearing my hair natural because this shower is about to steam the hell out of my hair and my press will be gone, but it was okay. We are here to get our hair wet anyway and there is no need to have a press. Once I finished showering I can hear Tony in the bedroom on the phone. I heard him say what do you mean he's been acting strange? What has he done mom? He must have realize that the shower was off at this point and he lowered his voice so I couldn't hear anything else. Damn, I wonder what his mother had to say and if it was their father she was speaking about. I really can't ask him because it was family business but something is not right because Tony is heated. I hurried and finished getting dressed and applying my oil and perfumes before exiting the bathroom. Like I suspected Tony had left the room and was now talking to Black by the front entrance. I made sure my hair was dry before I removed the towel from my head and I begin to brush it and applied my Carol's Daughter product to finish it off. There I was ready to go. I saw Justice coming from her room right as I was coming from mines. "You guys ready to go? Or do you have something more important than taking two beautiful ladies out?" I asked while walking towards them. They looked at us like damn but I can tell something was wrong. I pretended that I did not hear anything from the bathroom. "Are you guys okay" I asked. "Yeah we're good, just stunned by the beauty." Tony said before kissing me on the cheek. I can tell something was up but if he wanted to keep it to himself then that was fine with me. I was much shorter than Tony this time because I did not wear any heels with my outfit. I just decided on some flat sandals by Michael Kors. I can tell that Justice was not feeling the heels also, she had on some flats and a long sheer thin skirt with a halter top. This bitch can dress and it's no wonder we are family. We exited the room and the elevator ride down was quite. The men were looking angry but tried to make the best out of it. I can tell there was something going on and I had a feeling that this trip was going to be cut short. We got back in the limo and we were on our way to eat. We decided on The Palm since I heard it was the best place to eat. Once inside we were seated in the rear by the bar but also close to the window so that we were able to enjoy the view. The men were whispering among themselves and I finally said. "Okay, what seems to be the problem, you two have been acting like something is bothering you since we left the hotel. Is everything okay?" Tony and Black looked at me and Black gave Tony the okay to let us know what is going on. He didn't give us the full details but he said. "When you were in the shower my mom called and was telling me she was a little concern because our father was acting weird. She said she didn't understand it but she did notice that he was leaving the house every night at nine and not returning till eight in the morning. She also said he has been whispering on the phone and when she comes in the room he immediately disconnects the phone. She thinks something is up with him and she wants us to know what is going on. But I can't seem to understand. The only thing I can think of is either he has another family somewhere or he's up to no good. It's funny because he popped up from nowhere with this bullshit ass story talking about he been in hiding all this time. I thinks he set the whole situation up and had no intention of ever seeing us again but he has ran into some issue, but soon as we get back we will get the truth." Damn was all I can think but what was he hiding and what was he up too. I guess we will find out when we return. I tried to lighten the situation by making small talk but the men thoughts were elsewhere. "I thought this was going to be a special vacation, let's make the best of it." I said trying to remind the men why we were here. Justice didn't hear me because she was too busy going back and forth to the restroom. Now I'm wondering if she's okay. After finally being able to eat our food, we walked to a few stores and went back to the hotel suite. Tony was sitting on the bed and I closed the door. "So what do you want to do? Do you want to just cut the trip short and go back home to see what's going on? I asked Tony. He looked at me and said. "Lacy the last thing we want to do is cut the trip short but I think the best thing to do is to go home and check this out." I completely understand. Tony told Black the news and we were packing to catch the next flight back to Atlanta. They told us we can stay and they can return in a few days but we declined. Truthfully, all this bullshit is taking a toll and I am tired of it. Our flight did not leave until ten that night, so we were sitting in the airport for hours. Tony phone rung and it sounded like there was a problem now. He jumped up walked over to Black and said. "That was Miss Mae and she said momma is in the hospital. She said she overheard momma arguing with our so call father and he started beating her. She said she had to go and get security to pull him off her and by that time momma was unconscious and blood was everywhere. She said he's gone and that the police could not find him." Black was furious and I was surprised to hear this. Justice and I jumped up and the guys were looking for a private flight. We were told private jets can be rented at the beginning of the airport. The men could not wait three more hours for the flight and they had to get to their mom now. Once we arrived at the front of the airport Tony and Black paid for a private flight and we were on our way back to Atlanta. Tony was making phone calls to secure that we had cars waiting at the airport and Black was making calls to secure that there were guns available and goons there waiting also. Justice and I were pissed. Not because of the trip but because of Mrs. Lillian. She was so nice to us and approved of our relationship with her sons. We know how much they love their mother and how they kept her protected this long and it was the fool that put them in this life style that caused pain in her life not once but now twice. "When we arrive in Atlanta, there will be a car waiting for you ladies to take you to a secure place until we find this fool. Do not call us we will call you when it's done. We don't need anyone tracking your location. If you like you can go to your family house or this location. Either way we can have men keeping watch. You are still free to go as you please just with protection until this is resolved." Tony stated to us. I was okay with whatever. I hope they find that bastard. "If it's okay with you guys we would like to go with you to see your mom. We want to make sure that she's okay. And once I see that she is okay and that she will remain okay, we can leave if that's what you want." I told them. Little did we know this was the beginning to the end. Life was going to be very different. We landed in Atlanta less than two hours and they had called every goon in Atlanta. Since we were going to the same location which was Grady Hospital we rode in the same car. The drive to the hospital seemed longer than the flight. I guess because we were rushing. We were at Grady in no time and Miss Mae was waiting outside the emergency room when we arrived. She hugged the guys and explained to them that they were doing all they could but Mrs. Lillian's condition was worse than we thought. "They operating on her now and they said they will let us know as soon as they finish but right now they're doing all they can do. He beat her so badly and I tried to stop him but he slung me across the room so hard that I blacked out but when I came too, I immediately ran and got her guards to help her. It may have been too late, I don't know how long he beat her." Miss Mae stated with her head down. I can tell she was feeling bad.

Tony and Black were furious, they were going to find their father and make him pay but they didn't know where to start because he popped up from nowhere and came back in their lives. Before anyone can say anything Miss Mae handed Tony two big envelopes packed with stuff and said. "The other day when your father left, your mother talked to me. She told me if anything shall ever happen to her that I should give you these. She would not tell me what she was speaking on but she said you will know what to do. She said you and Black always handled things professionally." Tony grabbed the envelopes gave one to Black and we walked inside the emergency room behind Miss Mae. Tony was in tears and so was Black but that didn't keep Tony from saying what he had to say. "Miss Mae, I appreciate everything that you have done for my mother and I am sorry this had to happen to her and you. But I can assure you he will be found and he will pay for this. I know you have a family of your own and you don't have to stay here, as soon as we hear something I can call you with the update." Tony spoke to her directly like she was his mother away from his mother.

My heart felt so heavy and I didn't know what to do. I have never been placed in a situation like this before. All I can do is sit here and hope everything turns out fine. Miss Mae insisted on staying until Mrs. Lillian was out of surgery. We sat in the waiting room for hours and finally at about two ten in the morning, the doctors came out and asked for the immediate family of Lillian. Tony and Black walked back with the doctor through the doors.

Chapter 15 (Tony)

I can't believe this coward ass bastard had the nerves to put his hands on my mother. Something has to be wrong with him. Does he know he just signed his own death certificate and there will not be a body to have a funeral? I'm sitting in this damn hospital and all I can think about is why we didn't check up on his story. If my mother don't make it, I can't do nothing but blame myself. How could we have been so stupid and let this man walk right into our life not knowing where he came from and what he has been doing all these years. Trust no one, trust no one. Miss Mae gave us these packages, I hope they contain information about him. Because if I know my mother correctly as soon as she found out he was up to no good she had him investigated. She grew up in this game and she knew no one could be trusted no one. She told me she liked Lacy but don't trust her yet, not until you know that you really love her and that she really loves you. I can see that Black is ready to kill him and at this point it's whoever get to him first because I may be pulling the trigger on this fool. He has to be a fool to fuck with my mother that way. After sitting so long in the waiting room, the doctor came out and asked for the immediate family of Lillian. Black and I jumped up so fast, we went to the doctor. He ordered us to go someplace private so that he may discuss the surgery with us. I'm thinking she's okay, she's okay. But this nigga still must die. Once we got behind the double doors the doctor said. "I am sorry to inform you, but your mother passed a few minutes ago. We did everything that we could do but she was beaten so badly it caused internal bleeding in the head and we could not stop it. Again I am sorry for your loss. If you will like to see her body before we take her to the morgue, she has been cleaned up and I can take you to her." What the fuck my mother is dead, Black

fell to his knees and all I heard was
"NO......NO........NO, not my mother, anybody but my
mother, take me, take me!" I grabbed Black
embraced him and told the doctor. "If we can please
see her and say our goodbyes, I will arrange for her
body to be picked up tomorrow." We followed the
doctor to her room and there she laid all peaceful like
she was sleep. Her face was bruised but she was still
beautiful. We walked over to her bedside and the
doctor left us alone with her. "Mommy why? Why
didn't you tell us this earlier, we could have
prevented this from happening. I hate him for this
and I promise you he will pay. I love you so much
and I am going to miss you. I need you to watch over
me and Black and I promise you I am going to watch
over Black because he's all I got left. You will always
be in my heart and forever a part of me." I said to her
with my head laying on her chest. Black just stood
there in shock. He was hurt the most because he was

always the momma's boy, she loved him unconditionally. She loved me too but he was the one she held closer to her heart because he took it the hardest when our father disappeared. I got up placed the cover over her head and we walked out. My momma laying up in a hospital bed heading to the morgue was not supposed to happen like this, she was supposed to pass of old age. I can accept that but this I can't accept. He took my mother from me and my brother. Does he think that's okay? When we walked out into the waiting room I can tell Lacy, Justice and Miss Mae was waiting to hear the news. So I said it to them clearly. "My mother passed away a little while ago, she had internal bleeding that could not be stopped and she passed." Lacy ran and hugged me and Justice embraced Black. Miss Mae looked like she was in shock. I immediately released Lacy and grabbed Miss Mae right before she collapsed. She had been working for my mother since we moved to Atlanta and was one of her closes friends. "Miss Mae, Miss Mae! Wake up, can you hear me?" I yelled to her while fanning. "Can we get a doctor over here?" Black yelled out. That was the first I heard him say since he was on his knees. The doctors ran over got Miss Mae and ran some test on her. She's going to be okay she is just in shock but they are keeping her overnight for precautions. I left her a note letting her know to call me as soon as she is okay and I will need her to set up arrangements for my mother.

I know Miss Mae will know what to get and recommend. I can't seem to function because so much is going through my mind. I lost my mother because of this bastard and now Miss Mae is in the hospital. I am going to make sure she is alright because she is just like a second mother to me and my brother. It's time to do what we need to do in order to resolve this issue. Black, Justice, Lacy and I all jumped in the car and was headed to the house when my phone rang. It was an unknown number and everyone knows that I do not answer unknown numbers. If you want to talk to me then I need to know where you calling from. The phone rung at least five more times unknown and finally stopped. Someone must really be trying to contact me but they don't want me to know where they calling from.

Everyone was quite in the car on the ride back to the house. I guess hurt feeling have you second guessing life. Black had his head resting in his lap and Justice was rubbing his back. Lacy was laying on my shoulder with her arms wrapped around my arm. "Black." I heard Justice say. "I have something that I need to tell you. I was going to tell you after the trip because I wanted us to enjoy it. But since we back already I think now is a good time." Me and Lacy looked at each other and I can tell we were thinking the same thing, I just know this girl is not going to end it again with my brother at a time like this. We had no idea what she was going to say. "Justice maybe now is not a good time for what you have to tell Black." Lacy spoke up and said. Justice looked at Lacy and said. "Girl this is as good of a time as any time." Then she looked at Black and said. "Black, I love you and I wanted you to know that I am pregnant. I have known for a while now and I wanted to be sure so the doctor confirmed it the other day before we left for Miami. I was going to wait because I wanted it to be a surprise for you." Wow, Justice pregnant! That was great news but then it makes you think, they say when there is death there is life. I hope it's a girl. Black and Justice hugged for what seemed like eternity and then Black said. "Justice that's the best news I have heard all day and I am ready to be a dad. In the meantime you need to be cautious of what you eat and what you do cause this is our baby." We all laughed and this was the beginning of something that will last forever, at least for now. Black turned to Justice and said. "Actually Justice the reason we were going to Miami is because I wanted to ask you something." He pulled the ring box from his pocket and said to her. "I know we haven't known each other very long but I love you and I want to spend the rest of my life with you, will you be my wife for life?" Justice screamed and said a big ass "Yes, Black, yes Black I will." I was happy for them but all the excitement ended when my phone rang again but this time a number appeared. I didn't recognize the number but I answered anyway. "What's up? Who is this?" I can hear a television on in the background and someone breathing in the phone but no one said anything. And just when I was about to hang up, he spoke. "I don't know what to say about what happen. I loved your mother and I would never do anything to hurt her. But they told me if I didn't kill her then they will kill her, you and your brother and then me. I did it to protect you boys. I hope you can forgive me." Charlie pleaded on my other line. "Forgive you, forgive you! You took the only other person we ever loved after we thought we lost you. You should have come to us and we would have been aware of the situation and got it handled. Our mother is gone and you calling talking about forgiveness. You should have let them kill you cause when we find you, it's going to be a reunion you will never forget." I yelled in the phone before hanging up. Black was pissed and so was I.

When we got to the house we had the goons search the place and make sure it was safe to enter. Once inside I instructed the ladies to pack their items because they were going to a secure location to keep them safe. There was a war about to start and I was going to see to it this time that nigga is dead. There is no excuse for what was done to my mother. While the girls were packing me and Black sat in the office and reviewed the photos and documents that were in the packages my mother left for us. I can't believe what we were looking at. There were photos of my dad with another woman. There were also pictures of him with her and three children. He's been living a double life. I wonder now if he faked his own death, just to escape being with us.

My mom had all the information, their names, social security numbers and addresses. She had the daily schedules of every one of them. Looks like he has also been living in Georgia, right under our noses and we didn't even know. "Look bro, this nigga been low key for all these years raising another family and just said fuck us. Then he want to go and kill out mother. He has to die slow along with the rest of these people. I don't give a fuck who dying on these pictures." Black yelled out. I can tell he was ready. "Wait here's a letter from mom." I said before reading it aloud.

DEAR BOYS,

*IF YOU ARE READING THIS LETTER, THEN I AM NO LONGER
HERE. I LEFT THIS INFORMATION FOR YOU BECAUSE I KNEW
YOUR FATHER WAS UP TO SOME SHIT.*

*WE WERE HAPPY AT FIRST, HE STAYED EVERY NIGHT AND WE
WENT OUT AND HAD A GOOD TIME. BUT SOON HE WOULD
SNEAK OUTSIDE ON THE PHONE WHISPERING AND WHEN I
WOULD ASK HIM WHAT WAS GOING ON HE WOULD SAY,
"OH NOTHING JUST GO BACK IN THE HOUSE." FROM THAT
MOMENT ON I KNEW SOMETHING WAS NOT RIGHT. I HIRED
A PRIVATE DETECTIVE AND HAD HER FOLLOW HIM
WHENEVER HE LEFT.*

*I FOUND OUT THAT HE HAS BEEN LIVING IN GEORGIA SINCE
WE MOVED, ABOUT TWO YEARS LATER. HE HAS BEEN
DEALING WITH DRUGS AND IS STILL THE HEAD MAN IN
CHARGE. I ALSO FOUND OUT THAT HE MARRIED AGAIN. A
MUCH YOUNGER WOMAN AND THEY HAD THREE CHILDREN
TOGETHER. AND THIS IS THE REASON HE LEFT US.*

*SHE IS THE DAUGHTER OF THE SUPPLIER THAT HE WAS
USING AND WHEN HER FATHER FOUND OUT SHE WAS
PREGNANT BY HI. HE ORDERED YOUR FATHER TO ABANDON*

*US AND MARRY HER OR HE WILL KILL US ALL. AND YOUR
FATHER DID JUST THAT.*

*HE PLANNED A RAID OF OUR HOUSE SO THAT WE WOULD
ASSUME HE WAS DEAD. BUT HE RECENTLY SEEN YOU BOYS
AT THE CLUB AND HE RECOGNIZED YOU IMMEDIATELY.
THAT'S WHY HE WAS FOLLOWING YOU BOYS. HE WANTED
TO SEE YOU. HE IS STILL IN LOVE WITH ME BUT HAD TO DO
WHAT HE HAD TO DO TO PROTECT OUR FAMILY.*

*I APPRECIATE HIM FOR THAT, BUT I AM ALSO UPSET THAT
HE WILL EVEN THINK TO SLEEP WITH ANOTHER WOMAN. I
THOUGHT WE WERE AND WOULD FOREVER BE SOUL MATES.
I CONFRONTED THE WOMAN AND YOUR FATHER ONE DAY
IN THE STREETS. I CAN TELL THAT SHE WAS FURIOUS, SHE IS
A BEAUTIFUL WOMAN BUT SHE WILL NEVER BE ME AND I
BELIEVE THAT WAS THE BEGINNING OF THE END.*

*LATER THAT DAY HE CAME TO ME VERY UPSET SAYING THAT
I DIDN'T KNOW WHAT I JUST STARTED AND HE EXPLAINED
THE WHOLE STORY TO ME. I WAS PISSED AT THAT POINT.
HE ALSO TOLD ME THAT SHE DEMANDED THAT I BE KILLED
OR SHE WILL TELL HER FATHER WHAT HE HAS DONE TO HER.
HE ASKED ME TO LEAVE TOWN OR AT LEAST FAKE MY DEATH*

SO THAT NO HARM COULD BE BROUGHT TO ME OR YOU BOYS. I REFUSED!

I HAVE LEFT ONE HOME AND STARTED OVER BECAUSE OF THIS HOME WRECKER AND I REFUSE TO LEAVE ANOTHER ONE. I ADVISED YOUR FATHER TO DO WHAT HE THOUGHT WAS BEST AND HE LEFT. I KNOW THAT I WAS NOT GOING TO LET THEM RUN ME FROM MY HOME. I DID NOT TELL YOU BOYS BECAUSE DEEP DOWN I ASSUMED YOUR FATHER WILL NOT DO ANYTHING TO ME BUT I ALSO DID NOT WANT ANY THING TO BE DONE TO YOU. I HAVE LIVED MY LIFE AND I WANT YOU BOYS TO LIVE YOURS.

I GAVE YOU ALL THIS INFORMATION BECAUSE I KNOW IF I AM DEAD IT IS BECAUSE OF HIM, YOU WILL NOT ACCEPT THAT AND YOU WILL BE SEEKING REVENGE. I WANTED YOU TO KNOW THAT THE REVENGE IS DEEPER THAN HIM AND IF YOU ARE LOOKING TO KILL YOUR FATHER YOU MUST WIPE OUT THE WHOLE FAMILY AND HER FATHER AS WELL. YOU HAVE ALL THE INFORMATION ON YOUR FATHER, HIS WIFE AND HER FATHER. I HAVE THEIR WHOLE OPERATION IN THIS PACKAGE.

IF YOU CAN PLEASE MOVE ON AND UNDERSTAND THAT

YOUR MOTHER LOVES EACH OF YOU VERY MUCH AND TO KEEP AN EYE ON EACH OTHER BECAUSE YOU ARE ALL YOU GOT!

LOVE ALWAYS

MOMMY (MUAH)

Tears were falling from our eyes as we read the letter but hatred was in our hearts. Now that we know it's another family that we are dealing with, we have to plan this wisely. This nigga and this bitch must go. Her whole family is a wrap especially her father who changed our lives forever. Black and I finished up in the office and called every goon we could call in the Streets of Atlanta and Miami. We scheduled a meeting for tomorrow morning because we needed to execute this plan properly. It's the start of a tragedy and may they souls rest in hell.

Chapter 16

This day has been crazy, first the death of Mrs. Lillian and now we packing our things like we will not be returning to this home. I don't know what Toni and Black have planned but I refuse to be another body in the morgue. Hell I'm scared to attend the funeral. What have I gotten myself involved in? I guess you really never know a person until you live in their shoes.

Justice and I was literally running all over the place getting stuff together. Her stuff is not over here but she never really lived with Black, so she had nothing to worry about. I was just ready for the nightmare to be over. All I could think about is, are we next? Are we even safe at this point with the guys? And where will their mines be?

I was finish and we left in my car leaving the guys there at the house. Justice and I were in silence the whole ride to the hotel. We had to get the president suite and there was security all night and day to make sure that we were safe. The guys told us that they will call us in a few days once they get business handled. It had been days since we heard from the guys and I was starting to worry. "Do you think everything is okay? I mean it has been days and we haven't even heard from them." I asked Justice.

She was upset anyway because she had just told Black she was pregnant and at least he could do was call. "I don't know what to think, I mean the least they can do is call. I can't be up here in this shit. I'm sitting here pregnant and stressing. I didn't sign up for this mess but I sure as hell know how to get out of it." Justice said. She jumped up grabbed her bag and was heading towards the door. "What are you doing? You know it's not safe for us to just leave, someone could have been watching." I said to Justice. "Fuck that shit, if they were watching, they watched your car pull in, so I will be taking a town car back to my moms. I don't have time for this bullshit. Sitting day and night, waiting to see if I'm next on a goddamn hit list.

I just told the man I loved a few days ago I was pregnant. You think he bothered to check on me or to even say I'm done with this street shit; I have a family to raise. Fuck this shit Lacy, you may want to sit your high and mighty ass here and wait but I refuse." Justice said while yelling. I was taken aback by her statements, how in the fuck she gonna sit here and say that bullshit to me. So I yelled back at her ass, "What the fuck you mean high and mighty? Hell we've been getting the same shit together, I been making excuses for your ass when you bailed out on your nigga. The least you can do this time before you leave is make sure he's okay. I don't act no different with you then what I've been acting all my life. But as my cousin if you feel like that then you can just get the fuck on, don't worry about Lacy from this point on. Go fuck with them trifling ass cousins of yours." Justice opened the door and got the hell on. I can tell she was pissed but I was even more pissed. I felt the same way she did but what happen to holding it down until your man gets it solved. I don't even understand why I was hanging with her ass anyway.

As kids we were tight, but as we grew up and were hanging with other family members like Kela and Mesha she really changed. She would get mad because I wanted better things in life and didn't hang with her and them two fools. I learned my lesson, hell once you crossed me that was the end of it. One day when we were like eighteen, I was hanging with Mesha and my old friend Shanta. We hung with Mesha day and night and that was because I was trying to get hooked up with one of the sexiest man in hood. He was the truth, big time drug lord and everyone wanted him. He was young and had money beyond the ceiling. Well Mesha man, Dro was always with us too. Hell we was riding with them everywhere but it wasn't like I wanted to go every day. Mesha will call us to come and ride with them. On this particular day Dro wanted to drop Mesha off at home and take me and Shanta with him. I declined and he dropped me off too but Shanta stayed with him. I didn't think anything of it, so the next week we were sitting in the hood with him heading back to Mesha house to hang out. Shanta starting bragging about who she done fucked and I am naming all kinds of niggas and she just keep say no, no and no. So, finally as a joke I said well who is it Dro? She dropped her head and was like yes. I was pissed, this is my cousin's man and you fucking him like it's all good. I went off and I told Shanta I was going to tell Mesha, I had no choice. Shanta was my friend but Mesha is my cousin my family. I can't betray my family and my family won't betray me. At least that's what I thought. So the whole ride back to Mesha house I didn't say shit and Dro noticed that I was upset. So when we got out the car and was heading to the apartment I said to him. "Dro, that's fucked up what you did, how you betraying my cousin." He grabbed me and pushed me back saying. "What you talking about shawty? What I do?" I wasn't scared but I wanted him to know that I know. So I told him. "You fucking that white girl, that's what you did. And we hanging with you and Mesha. I have to tell my cousin." Dro was pissed but he was keeping it cool. "Man I ain't fucked that white girl, she lying. I ain't fucked her." Was all Dro could say. So we walked on in the house and Shanta and Mesha was sitting on the sofa. All I could say was this was a trifling bitch, she can sit here and fuck this girl man and sit in her face like nothing happen. I knew at that moment she could not be trusted and not to trust her around any nigga I fuck with. A man gonna be a man and that's why you have to have true friends that will not cross that bridge with your man. This one situation turned out to be the beginning of a whole lot of drama between me and them and I didn't even fuck the nigga. The next day my sister dropped me off at Mesha place and I was confronted by her and three more bitches, her so call friend Keisha and our cousin Trudy and our cousins girlfriend Shenell. Mesha was talking shit about her friend saw me last night all hugged up outside with Dro. We were kissing and hugging. I was like that was bullshit, he pushed me back because I confronted him about the white girl Shanta, I told him I was gonna tell but where was the bitch that told her that lie because I wanted to see what she had to say. Mesha was lying because the whole time it was Shenell that told her that. So I called my sister back and I left. Them hoes was not trying to fight me or anyone I told Mesha I am not a Jerry Springer hoe, I don't fuck my cousins men. She didn't want to hear it so they stop fucking with me and Justice was right in the middle of it too. She went back and told those lies and was ready to fight me when they were.

I was riding with the white girl Shantal one day and we rode right pass them because they were down the street at my aunties house. Well when we pulled in front of Shantal's house she was getting out to run in and get something, me and her sister Ria was staying in the car. Mesha pulled up with Shanell in the car and Justice and they jumped out. Mesha slapped the shit out of Shantal and I was like you better hit her ass back, but Shantal jumped back in the car and took off. I was furious because at the same time Shanell was challenging me to get out the car. And I was getting out when she pulled off and it threw me back in the seat and the door shut. I was like pull the fuck over I ain't scared of them bitches pull over. But as we were being chased by them it was also funny. Ria was so pissed at her sister, why didn't you hit that bitch back. We later pulled in front of a police station and a patrol car was dispatched to Shantal's house where she filed a police report that later had Mesha arrested. Later that night Shantal and I met up with Dro and his cousin that I fucked with on and off. And he was like, why your cousin slapped you. I told him she didn't slap me she slapped the shit out of Shantal. I am not worried about Mesha because if she wanted to fight me she would have that day I was in her apartment. But I didn't like the way Justice was on their side and we were first cousins they were only our third cousin and to me that didn't count. But that was the beginning of a whole lot of bullshit between me and my family.

I tried to forgive Justice and I did because I introduced her to a whole new playing field of life. We became close like we used to be. But I guess since I know how she truly feels about me it's back to square one. Lacy on her own again with no family and distance friends. I say distance because the friends I do have I haven't seen in a while but that's about to change because this Toni situation is probably a rap.

I got a note under the door from the hotel. It states that the bill for the week is past due and the account given to cover the charges is declining. I was in shock, so I decided to call Toni. I called his phone three times and there was no answer. Now I was starting to worry. I put my clothes in my luggage and decided I had to check out of this hotel. The man they sent with us to the hotel was gone, he may have walked Justice out. This was my opportunity to get ghost before he returns. I stopped at the front desk and paid the bill with my credit card since Tony card was declining. I didn't understand why his card was declining but I was about to find out. While the clerk was checking me out I asked if there was a rental company in the hotel. And with my luck it was. I needed to take a ride to see what was going on. Once I checked out I went over to the rental company and rented a vehicle with dark windows and it was time to find Tony. Something didn't feel right and I had to find out sooner than later. My life can't be on hold. While driving up the highway, I called Justice to see if she made it home safely. I know we have our differences but I had to be sure in this situation. "Hello!" Justice answered with an attitude. I looked at the phone before speaking and responded just as bad. "I was just checking to see if you made it home alright? I checked out of the hotel and I am heading to Tony's house. If I see Black I will let him know that he needs to call you." I can tell she didn't really care if he called her or not. We hung up and I was getting off the exit. I know Tony said to stay away until he calls but damn, how long did he want me to wait?   I rode slowly pass Tony house and I can see that nothing was out of the ordinary. The house looked normal. I rode pass Black house and nothing was out of the ordinary and his house also looked normal. What the fuck was going on? If everything looked normal than where could they be? I know their mom just died, so I decided to go see Miss Mae. I pulled up to Mrs. Lillian house and got out. The house seemed dark like emotional darkness. I rang the doorbell and Miss Mae answered the door. "Hello, Lacy! What brings you by here?" Miss Mae asked. I can tell she was hurt and I can see that she was getting Mrs. Lillian things packed. "Hey, Miss Mae, I was just coming by looking for Tony or Black. After we left the hospital, they told us to pack some clothes and check into a hotel and they will call us but they haven't. And Justice is upset because she just told Black she was pregnant and he haven't called. I rode pass the house and everything looks normal. Have you seen them or spoken to them?" I asked her hoping she can shed some light on the situation. Miss Mae took my hand and pulled me into the house and directed me to have a seat. "Lacy, I haven't seen them. When I came from the hospital the next day, Tony instructed me to have his mother buried. He had already paid the funeral home for everything. He said they had to go away for a while and handle this situation. He told me not to worry about any guest for the funeral. Just say my goodbyes because he and Black said theirs at the hospital. I was told to clear out her house and sell it. He gave me the deed to the house and said whatever I receive from it I can keep because I had been so good to his mother. He didn't want me to stay in the house because he didn't want me to be harmed. I just had Lillian buried yesterday and they didn't show up. I left Tony and Black a message letting them know of the location." I can't believe this, they have disappeared and didn't even have the courage to let us know.

I talked to Miss Mae for a few more minutes then I left. While riding back past Tony house I noticed the FBI had the place surrounded. So I parked the car and got out at the gate and watched. They came out with nothing but guns, no Tony and no Black. I saw the same agent that we talked to the night Tony and Black were arrested. I had to get out of the area before he sees me. I started walking back to my car but it was too late. He already saw me and I was stopped by some agents. He walks up to me with a big ass grin on his face. "Well, well, Miss Lacy Pierce. To what do I owe this honor? Do you know where your boyfriend is because we're looking for him? Do you remember the last time we spoke? You told me if I don't have a body, I don't have a murder charge. Well I have a body now and charges have been brought against your boyfriend for murder and drug charges. I advise you to call him and let him know to turn his self in as soon as possible." I looked at his country ass with disgust. This is not the time to fuck with me. "Look Mr. I want to hide behind my badge. Just because you have a body does not mean Tony killed the hoe. And I'm looking for Tony myself, let's just hope you find him before I do. I actually came by to pick up the rest of my things because we called it quits a week ago and he's been avoiding my calls." I told some lies to keep the agent out my face and to also get in the house. I know if I can get in I may be able find some clues to where Tony may have ran off to. Then the agent decided he will speak. "Unfortunately, Miss Pierce, this house and cars have been seized for illegal activities and until Tony goes to trial and prove his innocence no one can enter the property and remove anything." This is messed up. I have so much shit in that house that Tony bought me and what I brought in. I know good and damn well I might as well kiss that shit goodbye. Tony is MIA and I don't know when I will see him again. I just walked off to my car and pulled off. At least I still had my money in the bank. I don't even know about the account that Tony put money in for me. But I'm pretty sure they froze that account as well. I called Tony cellphone and still no answer so I left this message. "Hey Toney, its Lacy! I rode pass the house and saw agents searching the place and everything you own has been seized. I was told to inform you that they found the China bitch dead and you are now a suspect for murder and other charges. I also talked to Miss Mae. I just hope you and Black are safe and I just want you to know what ever happens that I love you and will always love you. I don't blame you for disappearing, but I just wish you would have told me. No matter how long it is, I will keep this same number just in case you decide to call. Be safe, I love you and I pray everything is fine." I hung up the phone and I knew Tony could tell I was crying

on the other end.

Chapter 17 (1 year later)

It's been a year since I last talked to Tony and I can say this year has went by slow. After going through that lifestyle it was time for me to bring it down a bit. I sold my Jaguar and got myself a Toyota Camry fully loaded. I just wanted to be an average girl. I had money saved before I met Toney and that was the money I was living off of. I was able to find a nice administrative job at another law firm in south Atlanta. I have dated a few men since Toney but no one has been able to compare. I go to bed some nights thinking about him and how I miss him so much. I just need closure. Just something that can tell me he's okay and safe. Justice and I haven't really talked that much since we left the hotel. Her mom told me that she lost the baby. Doctor said stress played a role in the miscarriage. I made it my business to call Toney and leave another message informing him of this so that he will tell Black. The

FBI finally stopped following me. I guess they thought Toney would show up to see me, but that never happened. My life was as simple as it can be. I worked from eight to five, went home and watched movies until I fell asleep to do it all over again. Today was going to be different from all days. I could just feel it. When I left work for the day. I walked to my car and sat in it for a while before pulling straight off. My phone started to ring, it was from a blocked number. "Hello!" no one said anything. "Hello, why are you playing on my phone? My time is precious!" I spoke in the phone. "Don't hang up." Tony spoke in the phone. I was excited and nervous and hurt at the same time. I wanted to question him but I knew I couldn't. Then he spoke these last words. "Lacy I want you to know I received every one of your messages. I am so sorry for leaving the way I did, I hope that you can forgive me one day.

I love you with all my heart and that's why I

had to let you go. My life has changed for the worse and this was no place for you. You have a future and I want you to live life. I'm sorry again and I will never forget you. Please live life!" Then the phone disconnected and once again, Toney was gone. My heart was broke all over again, but I received closure. I know one day I will be dating again and living a normal life with no worries. But it was going to be tough moving beyond Tony. I drove the rest of the way home in silence. No music or phone calls. I just wish that I could have told Tony how I felt as well but I knew he hung up before any more hurt could be done. This night was also different from any other night I spent alone. I laid on my patio floor and just gazed up at the stars thinking that although Tony is in a different place we both were able to see the same stars.

Chapter 18 (TONY)

As I stand here watching Lacy leave her job, I know I can't approach her like I want to. It's hard letting her go because I love her so much. I see the hurt in her face and she never looked so beautiful. I see this side of her that I have never seen before and that let me know it was time to let her go. I called her and did what I didn't want to do but I know that was the only way she will let go. Black and I have not left Georgia yet because we had unfinished business. I had to wait until he was able to perform the job we had to do for our mother and our freedom from these streets. Black lost a baby and his love. I lost out on life with Lacy. But like my mom said in her letter, we didn't have a choice we were born in this life. I watched Lacy pull off in tears and it was time for me to go. I walked back to the car where Black was waiting. Tonight was the night to end my father's life and his family. We've been watching him for months and he know it's not over. He should have just left us alone and continued to live his life. He knows the game just like the rest of us and his time in the game has expired. "She's gone!" I spoke to Black. Black looked at me and he can tell I was hurt. "You had to do what was right. She is not about this life and even if she was, it not your choice to bring her in. I'm sure she understands. But now is the time to do what we are here to do and move forward." Black words were right, but I know Lacy Pierce will make some man a very happy man someday just like she did me.

As the sun went down, Black and I met with the goons in an abandon warehouse. We had my father's whole operation in order. We didn't leave no page unturned or no door open. It was time to wipe his life out along with his family. We know the consequences and we are willing to risk it all. Once we do this there will be a hit on our heads. We gave orders and loaded up to head out.

Tonight was family night for them. And they all stayed home and sat in the family room watching movies and eating junk foods. This was something that I remember doing when we lived with my father as children. It was too late to turn back now. I have no sympathy for him his wife or his children. She made the call and she will die slow. Our goons had already started knocking his goons off one by one. We made sure to make the gun shots silent so the sounds wouldn't alert my father. Once they were all knocked off it was Black and my turn to go in and eliminate this family. We walked in with our mask on and let off a round. My father turned around and spoke. "Now boys, don't do this. I didn't have a choice, I was trying to protect you." We pulled our mask off since he already knew it was us. It didn't matter anyway because they all were going to die tonight. "You killed our mother, and for what? You betrayed us and you were upset. This bitch of yours sent a request. Did she not know that revenge was going to be gotten?" I yelled at his ass.

Then nothing more was said. My father stood up and opened his arms to receive his bullet. Black hit him one time quick in the head. Then he turned to the wife and hit her once in the head. The children were all huddled with each other and crying. Black turned his gun to them and I placed my arm across his to lower his gun. "Just like us, they didn't have a choice. They were born into this life." I whispered to Black. And we turned around and walked out. I couldn't hurt a child but I knew these kids will grow up and look for us, so we just better be prepared one day for the reunion. That was the last of Atlanta we will remember. Another state, another city. And once again new identities.

www.ingramcontent.com/pod-product-compliance
Lightning Source LLC
Chambersburg PA
CBHW070109030726
47506CB00002B/657